Stepsister
Sally

Stepsister Sally

HELEN F. DARINGER
Illustrated by Garrett Price

*Harcourt, Brace
and Company
New York*

Contents

Stepsister
Sally

Chapter 1

Gran's Secret

There was a quick sound of footsteps on the back porch, a twist of the doorknob.

"Guess what, Gran!" Sally halted in the doorway to take aim with her schoolbag at the kitchen stool. The aim fell short, and the bag slid with a thump to the floor. A red knitted tam followed, with more accurate aim. "You're absolutely going to be surprised."

"Provided I'm not carried off by pneumonia in the meantime," Grandmother Brown observed drily, lifting a hot pan lid with a corner of her blue-checkered apron. A long smudge of flour whitened one eyebrow and powdered her cheek.

Sally's foot lifted automatically to push the door

shut. It was a guarded push, for Gran couldn't
abide the sound of banging. She said if you banged
doors it was a sign you hadn't been properly
brought up.

"You'll positively be surprised," Sally announced a second time, tossing her stubby brown

in Doncaster, but that was long ago, when she was too little to remember. She wasn't even sure she could remember her mother, though sometimes when she was dusting the photograph in the silver frame on the mantelpi   in the parlor or when Gran said the kind of bubbling way she laughed put her in mind of her mother, or that her mother used to like to sing, then it seemed to Sally she could almost remember.

After her mother's death Father had sold their house. Gran had brought Sally home with her to Westfield, because a boarding house was no fit place for a small child, even if her father had had time to take care of her, which he hadn't, busy as he was obliged to be all day long at the store. A few times Sally and Gran had journeyed on the train to Doncaster to spend Sunday with Father, and summer before last they had visited him for a whole week.

Gran had not enjoyed it at the boarding house. She didn't like eating with so many strangers at table and she didn't like the choice you had to make after meals between shutting yourself up in your room or listening to so much *talk-talk-talk* in the living room or else going out to look in store windows or maybe to a motion picture. It was a poor choice either way. But Sally enjoyed the visit, every minute of it, and wished they might remain longer. That was because she was young, Gran told her. The older you get, the less satisfaction you take in being cooped up in somebody else's house, with somebody else's things around you.

For the past few weeks, however, Father himself had not been at the boarding house. At Christmas time he had bought a house and got married. If things had worked out right, he would have had Sally spend her Christmas vacation in Doncaster, to get acquainted with her new family before she came in June after the close of school to make her home with them.

For Father had married a whole family, and Sally had now not only a new mother but two brothers and a sister. Unfortunately there had been a case of measles in her class at school, and the principal had put the entire grade under quarantine, not to go to parties or Sunday school or motion pictures, and most emphatically not to ride on trains. Sally had asked him very particularly about trains.

At first she could hardly think about anything else except how like a party it would seem when she went to live in Doncaster, with so many people in the house all the time and everybody talking and laughing and getting into each other's way as you do when you play move-about games, like Spin-the-Plate and Going-to-Jerusalem. Most likely she would have to keep some of her belongings out of sight in the top drawer so little Robert couldn't get at them to break them, things like her string of red beads and the pale green bottle of lily of the valley toilet water sister Dorothy had sent her for a Christmas present.

Robert was three years old, Father had written on the back of the snapshot he enclosed in a letter. Sally liked little boys. She liked them almost better than little girls. They weren't afraid of dogs and caterpillars and they didn't screw up their faces to cry if you happened to hit a trifle too hard when you were pretending to tussle with them.

The other brother looked almost as tall as Father. His name was Donald and he was seventeen years old and a senior in high school. The only boy as old as Donald with whom Sally felt well acquainted was Ruth Martin's brother Steve. When Steve was in a good humor he might look over your homework to see if you had the right answers, or even let you strum on his guitar provided you were careful.

But Ruth said you just ought to see him when he was in a bad humor. And she said he got awfully cross whenever you asked questions, even plain ordinary ones like why wasn't he going to take Mabel to the dance instead of Janet, she was so much prettier, and who sent him the letter on the pink stationery? Sally intended to ask brother Donald no questions, however much she wished to know the answers. She'd have to find out in some other way.

In the snapshot Donald was standing in front of his mother, and only the top of her head was visible. Nevertheless Gran and Sally were both decidedly of the opinion that she must be especially nice—and nice-looking too. Otherwise Father would never have chosen her.

It was Dorothy to whom Sally most eagerly looked forward. To have a sister practically your own age—only a year older—would be like having your very best friend come to stay in your own house. You could help each other with your arithmetic problems and the dishwashing and walk arm in arm to school and have secrets together.

You might even have dresses alike and people who didn't know would inquire whether you were twins. Anyhow, even though Dorothy's hair should turn out to be blond, as Gran surmised from the picture, people couldn't help knowing you were sisters.

For a time Sally's homework suffered because she spent so much time thinking about her new family. Once during an oral test on the presidents when the teacher asked who had been responsible for the Louisiana Purchase, she replied hastily, "Not me." At which everyone laughed. The teacher smiled too, for she could tell from Sally's dazed expression that she had been caught daydreaming. Ordinarily history was one of her best subjects.

As January advanced, Dorothy and Doncaster receded. There was extra homework because the end of the term was approaching, a fresh snowfall made coasting especially good on the steep slope of Barclay's pasture, and whenever there was time, which was hardly ever, Sally and Ruth had to practice a piano duet, *Meditation*. Mrs. Martin planned to have them play it when the D.A.R. met at her house next month. . . . So now Sally's "Who's coming? Not Father?" was less a query about him than why Gran was having chicken for supper.

"Nobody's coming," Gran replied, turning out a second pan of cookies to cool on a clean white dishcloth. "Somebody's going."

"Has somebody invited us for Sunday dinner?" The crisp sugary smell was irresistible. Sally sampled two broken halves. "The Longs, I hope. They always have ice cream."

"No," said Gran. "And not we. You."

Something in her voice, in the steadiness with which the faded blue eyes looked out from their smiling wrinkles, struck Sally. "You're keeping a secret from me, Gran!" She was certain of it, but not altogether certain it was the pleasant kind of secret her grandmother's usually were.

"It won't be a secret for long." Gran busied herself at the sink. "Your father telephoned this morning. Long distance."

Above the swish of dishmop, the spray of hot water against mixing bowls and pans, Sally's quick ear detected a familiar overtone. The secret must be extra special, because Gran was trying to make believe it was just ordinary, to tease her. Sally's curiosity kindled.

"What'd he say? Was it anything about me?" She was almost sure it had been.

"He said Monday is the beginning of a new school term," Gran reported, scraping a knife along the cooky cutter where the dough had stuck.

"But everybody knows that already," protested Sally. "That's why we were let out early this afternoon." Really, Gran could be too provoking, acting so calm and innocent. "What else did he say, Grannie Brown?" she urged. "Tell me!"

"He said he and Julia had been talking it over and they don't see why you couldn't just as well change schools now as wait till September."

"Oh." Whatever Sally may have expected by way of surprise, she had not expected this. "Oh," she said again, blankly. She felt as she had once at the boarding house when she wakened suddenly in the middle of the night and couldn't remember where she was. "What did you tell him, Gran?"

"I told him he couldn't expect me to be enthusiastic about sending my only grandchild off in such a hurry, when I'd been counting on June." She rinsed out the dishmop, squeezed it thoroughly, and then let it slip back into the water. "But you're his daughter and he has first claim. Besides," she added briskly to counter the dismay that was beginning to show in the depths of Sally's brown eyes, "as I said to him, the best place for young folks to grow up is with other young folks, and the sooner the better for all concerned."

"But I can't," protested Sally. "Not next term. I've been 'lected captain of our basketball team."

"Captain! Well, well, Sarah Brown, I'm proud of you." Even Rufus, who had returned unobserved to curl up in a corner behind the stove, could hardly have failed to appreciate the surprise and pride in Gran's voice, except of course that he had already gone back to sleep.

"Your father'll be pleased. He used to play basketball. But now you've good reason to let someone else enjoy being elected."

"In Doncaster I mightn't have a chance to play," Sally reminded her grandmother. "Lots of places don't have basketball till high school." But her objection was weakening. Already her thoughts were turning toward Dorothy.

"Yes, if anyone was to ask me," Gran replied from the pantry (it may be that she had misunderstood what Sally said), "I'd certainly have to call you an uncommonly lucky girl." She spoke a trifle loudly, above the clink of the pans she was setting away.

Suddenly Sally began to feel as cheerful as Gran sounded—as if tomorrow were her birthday, with the layer cake already baked waiting to have the icing spread on and the holders stuck in place for the slim pink candles. And when she went clattering down the basement steps to sort her things, to see what to carry with her on the train, what to leave behind for Gran to send, she seemed to herself to be floating like a feather above the thwacking sound of her shoes.

"My skates, of course," she called up the stairs a moment later. "They're new. Do you think I should take my sled, Gran? And what about my stilts?"

Her grandmother vetoed both, the sled because it would cost more than it was worth to send, the stilts because if there wasn't lumber enough in the hardware store to make a pair of stilts, the family might as well move right away to the poorhouse. Besides, in a town the size of Doncaster it might be thought that a girl as old as Sally was getting too big for such tomboyish games.

The basement belongings attended to, Sally dashed upstairs to her room to lay out a few special possessions for Gran to tuck into the corners of the suitcase Gran had already packed. Her auto-

graph album, the pale green bottle of toilet water
—and of course it would never do to allow the
yellow china piggy bank to be sent parcel post
with the rest of her things. Mr. Martin had
brought the bank from the five-and-ten cent store
in Indianapolis when she was seven years old, one
for Ruth and one for her, and she had had it ever
since.

She held the bank to her ear and shook it. Usually she knew exactly how much money there was
inside, but this time she wasn't sure. She rummaged in the top drawer for a nail file. If you
inserted the file in the slit (the thin blade of one
of Gran's old kitchen knives was better, but there
wasn't time to go downstairs) and then turned the
bank upside down and shook it carefully, and kept
on shaking, you could get the money out, one coin
at a time. . . . Twelve pennies and a nickel. You
can do a lot with seventeen cents. But she did not
intend to spend it now, she had only taken it out
to count.

"If you're going to tell the neighbors good-bye,
you'd best be at it," Gran warned from the foot of
the stairs. "It's already dark outside, and supper's
within a few minutes of the table. And don't forget to turn out the light in your room."

The Smiths were quite as astonished as Sally herself had been to learn that she was departing on the morning train for Doncaster. Mr. Smith laid down the newspaper he was reading to talk with her, and his wife turned the burners low so the cooking could take care of itself while she came in from the kitchen to hear the particulars. The Smiths were the youngest people in the neighborhood; that is, the youngest married ones. For more than a year they had lived next door, and their baby was two months old.

Mrs. Smith declared that Johnny (she meant her husband, not the baby; she always called it "Precious" or "Lambikin") would certainly miss Sally's entertaining company. She herself didn't know how she'd ever manage the housekeeping without her to depend on in an emergency, to run to the grocer's. And now who would stay with the baby after school on days when Mrs. Smith had to go shopping? For she wouldn't trust anybody and everybody with her lamb, indeed she wouldn't!

Mr. Smith was of the opinion that the only solution was for him to move his family right along with Sally—lock, stock, and barrel. Did she think the hardware store could use an extra clerk? Of course she knew he didn't mean it—at least not the part about moving—but she pretended to take him seriously and promised to use her influence with her father.

Both the Smiths accompanied her into the next room to see the baby asleep in his crib. They would have waked him up to say good-bye, but Sally would not allow it. Sometimes she felt older than both of them put together, they seemed so inexperienced about babies.

Before she crossed over to the Walkers' she stopped in the middle of the street to look back at the Smith house. She certainly hoped they'd make out all right with the baby.

The air felt smooth as a piece of ice you hold to your cheek in summertime. Under the corner street lamp the new-fallen snow shone with a radiance like moonlight, but along the uncleared sidewalk and on the lawns it was shadowed with bare tree branches. Sally didn't think she had ever before noticed how high the trees reached, with nothing but sky above, where pale stars showed. It was like coming unexpectedly into a new world, with only the lighted windowpanes in the dark houses to remind you of the old one. When she was in the lower grades she used to have the same feeling when she read a fairy book—as if a door had opened and she were entering to take her place with the golden-haired princesses in the crystal palace. She sighed a little, remembering the enchanted wonder of the fairy palace.

The Walkers had finished supper. They always had it early because Mrs. Walker said the only time in the day she could sit down to rest herself and read the morning paper was after she had got the family fed and the kitchen tidied and the two youngest packed off upstairs to bed. Sometimes she got a day or two behind with the paper, there was so much to do. She was washing dishes when Sally knocked at the back door.

"Go right on into the dining room," she told her. "Zelda's gone next door to see if she can borrow a postage stamp. There's not a one in the house and Teresa wants to write a letter. You can talk to the boys till she gets back."

Alex and Andy, who were both in the fourth grade although Alex was the older by a year, were arguing over a checkerboard at one end of the dining table. Behind them, mounted on chairs turned upside down, Stanley and Reggie spurred their wooden steeds in headlong race. Above the clamor Sally could hear Teresa playing *Humoresque* on the piano in the front room. Teresa wouldn't practice finger exercises, she always played pieces. She was temperamental, her mother said, and you have to handle temperament with gloves on. It won't do to force it.

Sally was somewhat relieved not to have to carry on a conversation with Teresa. Whether it was because she was temperamental or for some other reason, she often made you feel uncomfortable. Zelda wasn't at all like her big sister. Zelda was plump and good-natured and harum-scarum, and you could always have a good time with her.

The struggle for the checkerboard ended with Alex in possession. "C'mon, play with me," he invited Sally. "Andy's no good. It takes him all day to make a move."

She couldn't, she explained, she'd just come to see Zelda and tell her good-bye. Tomorrow she was going to Doncaster.

Teresa, who must not have been attending with both ears to her music, joined them. "Cinderella!" She said it with a smile, but not the sort which invites a smile in return. Sometimes when Rufus was watching the wrens in the grape arbor he pulled his lips back like that.

"So poor little orphan Cinderella's going to take up her abode with her cruel stepmother and ugly stepsisters," she continued, posturing to suggest one of the sisters preening before a mirror.

Most people, except Gran, considered Teresa pretty. Gran said she'd prefer straight hair and a pleasant disposition any day. Then, dropping the rôle of actress to speak in a more natural manner, Teresa added, "Don't forget us, Sally. Don't consign your old friends to the limbo of oblivion." Ever since Teresa had been in high school she had affected long words.

Sally didn't say anything. She couldn't think of anything to say. She knew Teresa meant it for a joke about Cinderella, yet she somehow could not make herself laugh or answer back. There was a kind of spreading numbness within her, as though a fire where she had been warming herself had gone out.

"Back already?" Gran was astonished to have her return so soon. "I thought it would take you a good half hour to make the rounds of the Longs and the Tiltons and the Dagues and the—"

"I didn't," said Sally. "Just two places."

Gran gave her a sharp look. "Did you see Zelda?"

"She wasn't at home." Sally's voice sounded

muffled, probably because she was taking off her rubbers. "Teresa was there."

"Humph!" The ejaculation may have been intended to express Gran's opinion of Rufus, who was at the moment twining his black length around her ankles in fawning devotion. "If you make me spill the chicken before I get the platter to the table," she threatened, attempting to push him aside with her foot, "you'll spend the rest of the winter outside in the cold. Nor you needn't miaow at me like that. You're not hurt and you very well know you're not."

Rufus sought balm for his ruffled pride from Sally, who gave him a perfunctory pat.

"You needn't hang up your coat," Gran told her. "Just leave it on the chair where I'll be sure to see it. It may need a few stitches in the lining. If your father weren't in such a hurry you wouldn't have to start off in an old coat. I was waiting for the February sales." With a single deft movement she scooped a little hollow in the mashed potatoes and set a lump of butter there. "On the other hand, most likely it's a good thing we haven't bought a new one. There'll be a better selection in Doncaster, and your new mother will no doubt have ideas of her own about what's fashionable."

Without seeming to, her blue eyes were studying Sally's face trying to read the cause of her
silence. "Ruth telephoned while you were out, to
know about the game."

"Did you tell her? About me, I mean?" The
question conveyed no real interest.

"Did I!" Gran was as lively as Sally was list-
less. "I wish you could have heard her. Almost
pulled the receiver out, she was so upset. Said
they couldn't get along without you, you were the
best player on the team, she'd be lost without you,
you were the very best friend she ever had, there
was nobody like you for good times, and more of
the same until I was afraid the chicken would be
scorched to a cinder before I could get back to the
stove."

Sally lifted her head. "After supper I'll call
her."

" 'T won't be any use. Anybody who attempts to
call the Martins this evening will get nothing but
a busy signal. I hope her father isn't intending to
sell insurance over the phone tonight, because if
he is, he's in for a disappointment." Gran chuckled
a little, as at some private joke. "His youngest
daughter will be glued to the phone box. She told

me she was going to call up everybody in your
class so they could all—"

Gran broke off with a self-accusing, "There now,
I all but told."

"Told what, Gran?" Sally's face had bright-
ened. "Tell me, Grannie Brown!" she demanded
with a measure of her accustomed eagerness.

"I've gone so far you can't help guessing. I
ought to set a guard on my tongue, letting slip
what I shouldn't! The whole class will be at the
train to see you off."

Her grandmother looked so contrite at spoiling
the surprise, Sally had to cheer her up by promising to act so astounded they'd never in the world
dream she had even suspected. Honestly, she told
Gran, and it seemed to relieve Gran's conscience
of quite a load, honestly she was glad to find out
ahead of time. It would give her a chance to think
what to say. Because when you haven't suspected
in advance about a surprise, you usually just stand
there like a dummy.

She had eaten her mashed potatoes and finished
with the wishbone (with the latter she had had
surreptitious assistance from Rufus, to whom Gran
had granted the privilege of the dining room for
the occasion) and was just about to reach for an-

other dumpling and a little more of the stewed corn, when something occurred to her. "How'll you manage after I'm gone, Grannie? Won't you be afraid to stay all alone?"

Not afraid, her grandmother replied, but certainly she would be lonesome. She might go to Santa Barbara to stay with Martha. Martha had been urging her this long time to come to California.

Aunt Martha was Gran's sister, and she had two big orange trees in her own back yard. That Gran should travel all the way to California without Sally, that she should stand under the trees and pick oranges for herself when Sally had never so much as seen an orange tree except the tiny one in the pot in Mr. Hill's greenhouse, was a prospect hardly to be borne.

Until that moment Sally had not thought how it would be not to have Gran. Whenever she imagined herself with her new family, Gran was always somewhere within reach in the background, if not actually visible. And the new home she pictured herself living in bore a comfortable resemblance to Gran's house, except that it was larger to hold more people.

"But you can't go," she pointed out in a rather

hopeless attempt to dissuade her grandmother. She felt hollow in the pit of her stomach, a kind of emptiness not to be assuaged with mashed potatoes and dumplings. "What would become of Rufus?"

"You needn't fret yourself about that gentleman. The neighbors will look after him," Gran replied easily. "No doubt he'll be fatter and lazier than ever, by the time I get back."

So Gran wasn't planning to stay always in California. The hollowness in Sally's middle began to shrink in size. "You may have to put him through a course of training to cure him of his dormouse habits," Gran continued. "It's not good for a cat to spend all his time eating and sleeping."

"But I'll not be here." Sally hoped Gran would contradict her. And Gran did. Promptly.

"Not be here!" She sounded really indignant. "You and Dorothy will both be here, visiting. Summertime's no time for a city. You'll both be needing fresh country air."

Except for some uncertainty about Dorothy, Sally was beginning to feel rather cheerful again. "Dorothy mayn't want to come to a little place like Westfield," she said doubtfully. "She mightn't like it here."

Gran scouted the notion. "Not like Westfield?

Of course she'll like it. Just you wait until she hears about the picnics we have in Westfield, and the Sunday-school camp in the grove by the river, and all your friends waiting to be friends with her, and the parties, and going to your Uncle Tracy's to help with the threshing dinner. I shouldn't be surprised if she tries to persuade your father to move the whole family here."

"Some of 'em would have to sleep in the barn," Sally giggled, taking another dumpling on her plate. "Maybe you ought right away build a wing on the house, Gran."

Gran would not let her help with the dishwashing. They'd rinse and stack the dishes in the sink to wait till later. Sally had to run next door to bid Mrs. Shoup good-bye because she was old and ailing and might have her feelings hurt if there wasn't time to see her in the morning. Then she had to polish her shoes, her school pair as well as her Sunday ones. While she worked at the shoes, Gran ironed a few things she had washed out at the last minute.

"You may not have happened to notice about your father, seeing him so seldom," Gran told her, "but he's absent-minded at times. Even as a small boy he used sometimes to go off in a brown study whilst everyone else around was playing or talking. He's a kind man, your father, but he's not very observant." Her manner was so sober that Sally stopped squeezing the tube of shoe polish to look at her.

"Your mother was a good wife for him because she was quick to notice, and she helped him see things with her eyes. Helped in such a quiet way I doubt he was aware of it. Little things mostly, like whether one of his clerks wasn't feeling left out because nobody was talking to him when they had them all at the house for evening dinner.

"Full of fun your mother was too, and that was good for your father." Gran shook out one of Sally's blouses and would have ironed it all over again a second time if Sally had not stopped her. "Talk about absent-mindedness! I'm tarred with the same brush," she exclaimed ruefully, folding up the blouse again ready to pack. "How shall I ever manage without you?" There was a smile on her face but Sally knew she meant it seriously. "You're your mother's own daughter for noticing things, though in some respects you remind me of your father. I trust you, Sarah Brown."

Gran always said "I trust you" whenever Sally was worried for fear she might fail in an arithmetic test or not be able to make a basket when it came her turn to throw for goal, or fretted lest she might forget part of the piece she had to play at a recital or the speech she had to make in assembly. It always made Sally feel better to hear Gran say it, even though sometimes she suspected her of only trying to cheer her up.

To know that somebody like Gran trusts you, makes you feel almost sure you won't fail if you try hard enough, even though you may make mistakes. Everyone makes mistakes of one sort or another, Gran said, even the wisest and best of people. The important thing is, not to make the same mistake twice.

This time, however, the words did not so much hearten Sally (indeed, she needed no heartening, being already quite happy, not to say excited) as make her feel responsible. Responsible for what, she could hardly have told. But she almost wished Gran hadn't said anything about trusting her.

Chapter 2

The Nick of Time

Long before the train pulled into Doncaster station, indeed long before it had reached the outermost fringes of the town, Sally had her hat and coat on, ready to get off. The hat was navy blue, with a rolling brim and a jaunty scarlet quill. Sally was partial to red.

The chicken sandwich left over from lunch she stowed in her coat pocket. The crumbs from the other sandwiches, the empty paper cup, crumpled napkins, waxed-paper wrappings from deviled egg and sweet pickle and cherry tart, she brushed into the empty lunch box, capping it neatly with the lid she raked out from under the seat where it had fallen. She set the box under the window where they wouldn't overlook it when they swept the car.

Skates balanced across her shoulder, the tissue-wrapped shoe box of cookies Gran was sending Father on her lap, she counted the money in her red leather pocketbook to make certain none was missing before she put her gloves on. Then she pushed the suitcase a few inches farther out into the aisle, not far enough to trip anyone but sufficiently to catch the brakeman's eye. At the preceding station he had lifted the grip down from the rack, but that was some time ago and it might have slipped his mind.

Alternately scanning the aisle for the brakeman and watching out the window for the station, she kept sedately to her place on the edge of the plush-upholstered seat. Although she was in a great hurry and the train persisted in poking along as if it had all week to get there, she remained quite calm except for a fluttering sensation in her chest. When you have ridden on trains before, you know what to do and aren't excited even though you are traveling alone.

There were but few people to meet the train, she saw when she stepped down beside her suitcase on the platform. She looked in vain for her family. It was a relief suddenly to remember that this was Saturday. Of course Father would have to be at the store to tend to the customers. But none of the ladies in sight had with her a little boy who might be Robert, and even if he had been left at home none of them so much as glanced toward Sally. And while the soot was still showering down from the engine on the murky piles of snow along the platform edge, the various ladies one by one attached themselves to someone else and departed.

Sally was beginning to wonder somewhat anxiously whether she ought to remain where she was until someone came for her or whether she should telephone the hardware store or perhaps ask the station agent where 1018 Lafayette Street was. If it wasn't too far she could easily walk. Only she couldn't leave her suitcase, which was too heavy to lug more than a few steps.

Two girls came around the end of a baggage truck. One was dark-haired, the other fair. The fair-haired one spoke. "Is your name Sally Brown?"

Sally assured her it was. "I'm Dorothy," she announced, and before Sally could say anything, "I've come to meet you. My mother said to tell you she's sorry but she can't meet you because she

has to work in the store today because the bookkeeper's sick in bed."

So that was why. It brought easement of mind
to hear. Sally's disappointment dwindled, leaving
scarcely more than a trace. Of course a hardware
store can't run without a bookkeeper. She would
have told Dorothy her mother needn't feel sorry,
it couldn't be helped, and she was awfully pleased
to make Dorothy's acquaintance, except that Dorothy continued talking. "This is my friend Mildred
Stone." The dark-haired girl nodded remotely. "Is
this your suitcase?"

Sally said it was. "Mother said to leave it with
the baggage man. My brother Don can get it later.
We'll walk. It's only five blocks."

If somebody would help, Sally thought they
could manage the suitcase between them, to save
Dorothy's brother the trouble. Ignoring the suggestion—or perhaps not hearing it, since she was
not looking at Sally—Dorothy summoned a boy.
She handed him a dime, Sally observed, handed it
out with such an air of grown-up competence Sally
felt years younger, as small as if she had been
dwarfed. In Westfield a nickel would be plenty
to give a boy about your own size to take your grip

across the platform to the baggage room. But she did not comment on it to Dorothy.

On account of the snow there was not room to walk three abreast on the sidewalk. Dorothy and Mildred went first because they knew the way. Besides, if Sally wouldn't think them too unutterably rude for words, they needed to discuss their Sunday-school class play. They had had to leave in the midst of rehearsal to come to the station.

Sally said my goodness, no, she'd enjoy hearing about the play herself. Her school gave one every spring and they were lots of fun. But whether it was that the icy walks required her to watch where she stepped, or that the girls dropped their voices, she heard little of the discussion. She oughtn't have come today, she told herself uncomfortably, she should have waited. Whatever must Dorothy think of her for making her miss the rehearsal? Most likely she had the most important part, with such wavy blond hair and long eyelashes. She was stylish too. Nobody in Westfield had a coat with a velveteen collar. . . . If Sally had realized about the rehearsal she could just as well not have come until tomorrow—except that the train didn't run on Sundays. She would have liked to explain about the train, but the two were consulting almost in whispers now and kept walking faster and faster.

Mildred waited at the foot of the stairs while Dorothy showed Sally to her room. It was a small room but everything in it was new, as Dorothy pointed out, dressing table, chair, low table for writing and studying, and narrow bed, all of birch finished to look exactly like mahogany.

"You're the only one who got any new furniture," she told Sally, "except some new pieces Mother and Dad got for themselves. The rest of us just have to get along with what we already had."

Sally praised the furniture with rather more politeness than enthusiasm. It was not that she did not admire it. Quite the contrary—she admired it exceedingly. The mahogany finish was so smooth and shiny, the mirror so brightly new, the little writing table wholly unexpected and desirable. At Gran's she always used the dining table or the one in the living room, unless Ruth came over to make maps or a scrapbook and they spread out their things on the living room rug to have more room. She had never dreamed of owning a table specially to write on, and everything brand new. All of Gran's furniture was old; she'd had it ever so long.

But something, perhaps not so much what Dorothy said as how she said it, made Sally acutely aware how unjust it was that she should have four new pieces, while Dorothy, whose house it was, had none. Had it been Ruth or another of Sally's friends, Sally would have offered quick as a wink to divide up, half and half, or take turns, share and share alike. It's no fun having something if it makes someone not like you. She was ill at ease, as though she were to blame, though she knew of course that Dorothy didn't mean to make her feel guilty.

"It's the shiniest table ever to step out of a furniture store on four legs." She tried to make the words lively. "And a pink tufted bedspread! All of Gran's are plain white."

"This is my woom." A small boy, his blue blouse and blond hair equally rumpled, planted himself in the doorway to stare at Sally.

"It's not your room, Bobby, you know it's not. He kept his toys here when it was empty," Dorothy explained.

"After Mother went to the hardware store Mildred came for me, and I just had to go. I don't think he's too little to stay alone, do you? Run away now, Bobby, and play."

"It is so my woom. Me and Fido hasn't dot any woom. She's dot it." His blue eyes accused the newcomer.

"Don't pay any attention to him," Dorothy advised Sally. "Nor don't let him play in here. He's awfully messy. Go wash your hands, Bobby, they're dirty."

For a moment, sufficiently long to convey his defiance of big-sisterly authority, he maintained his position, feet planted wide apart, chin elevated in the air. Then, before a second reproof could follow, he turned and ran.

Dorothy stepped to the mirror to set her hat straight. The hat was dark red, like her coat, a color Gran would call wine red. It was a shade Sally was particularly fond of, though she'd never had a hat or coat of it.

"Ready, Dorrie?" Mildred called from the foot of the stairway.

"Please don't stay any longer on my account." Sally was chagrined to think it hadn't occurred to her earlier that the two must return to rehearsal. "I've loads to keep me busy, unpacking and all. Besides, I ought to write to Gran to let her know I arrived safely. It was good of you to leave the play to come to the station."

"Oh, that's all right. I was glad to do it. You're sure you won't mind? Because if you do, I'll not go." But she was drawing on her gloves. "Mother was afraid you might be lonesome."

No indeed, Sally assured her, she wouldn't mind staying alone. Really, Dorothy ought not hold up the play a minute longer; it wasn't fair to the others in the cast.

"You won't think I'm neglecting you?" Dorothy's smile of parting was somewhat abbreviated by her haste to rejoin Mildred. She was halfway downstairs before Sally could reply. As the front door banged shut, echoes of their voices and laughter floated upward through the silent house.

Slowly Sally lifted off her hat, pressed up a dented place in the crown and blew a speck of train dust from the feather. She laid the hat on the shelf in the empty closet and hung her coat on a wooden hanger beneath it. She'd be glad when she got a new coat. This one was rubbed shiny at the cuffs and the sleeves didn't come all the way over her wrists and it was much too short, she'd grown so fast.

Not until she closed the closet door did she remember that she hadn't anything to unpack, her suitcase was still at the station. She stood at the window to look out, careful not to lean against the white ruffled curtains. A strip of snowy side yard, a crooked plum tree black against a gray sky, smoke from a neighbor's chimney rising in a thin wavery column met her eyes, but it was not these she saw.

What she saw was Gran's kitchen. A long shaft of sunlight lay across the floor, gilding the green-and-white linoleum from window to hard-bottomed chair where Rufus slept, a sleek black ball. Gran was kneading bread at the table, her sleeves rolled up and her hands all floury. The room smelled of cinnamon and melted butter for cinnamon rolls, and bananas ripening on a pantry shelf, and ever so faintly of soap from the freshly scrubbed floor. It was a homey smell, warm and welcoming when you came in from the windy outdoors.

If she had a piece of paper she would write Gran a letter to tell her about the train trip and that Dorothy and Mildred had come to meet her because the others were busy at the store. But her box of stationery, a Christmas gift from Aunt Martha, was locked in the suitcase at the railroad station. Sometimes there was a piece in her pocketbook, but not today.

She pulled open the top drawer of the dressing table to put her purse away. The drawer was lined with pink-and-blue striped paper, out of a wall-paper sample book. Once Father had brought Gran a sample book, and she had let Sally and Ruth pick out the prettiest pages to keep for themselves and some to give away, as many as they wished.

Sally wondered how many rooms there were up-stairs besides hers, but she supposed she ought not investigate, at least not until she was better acquainted. Gran had her opinion of girls who went nosing around in other people's houses as if they belonged to them. On the whole Sally shared Gran's opinion, though perhaps less strongly. If any of the doors happened to be open on her way downstairs she didn't see what harm there would be in just glancing inside, so long as she didn't actually stick her head or feet in.

She settled herself on a green-upholstered chair by the widest of the living room windows, where she could watch for the family to come home. But the minutes were slow and she was too restless to sit long. She took turns trying the view from the two side windows and playing parts of *Meditation* and *My Old Kentucky Home* and *My Country*

'Tis of Thee on the piano—softly, not to disturb anyone who might happen to be upstairs. It was growing dusk, else she might have put on her wraps and gone outdoors to look around.

The house was so quiet, the shadows were creeping so stealthily toward her from walls and corners, she could not help feeling lonesome, a discouraged feeling, like that you have when you dream you are giving a party and nobody comes. As she stood by the front door, forehead pressed against the cold leaded pane, she was beginning to be sorry for herself. She wished she hadn't come, she wished she had stayed in Westfield. Nobody in Doncaster cared what became of her.

Through her dejection the sound of water gradually seeped—drip drip *drop,* drip *drop,* drip drop *splash.* Someone must have left a faucet turned on. She made her way to the kitchen. It was too dark to locate the light switch but the white enamel sink was plainly visible through the gloom. Neither faucet was leaking; she tried them both. There must be another spigot somewhere, maybe in the pantry or basement.

"Muvver!" A childish treble shrilled faintly from somewhere overhead. "Muvver, come quick! It's detting wet."

In her haste Sally barked her shin against a chair and bumped her head, but she was hardly conscious of it. Guided by the increasing volume of Bobby's voice, she groped through the dark upper hall.

"Open the door, Bobby! Let me in." She pounded with both fists against the closed door. He might be drowning, he might already be dead.

Under her feet the hall carpet squushed soggily as she renewed her pounding. "Open the door, I say!"

"I tan't." The voice was considerably less shrill, but there was no doubt the child was still alive. "The wivver'd wun out."

She fumbled for the doorknob, rattling it to enforce her command. "Let me in, I say!" Unexpectedly the door swung open (it had not been locked) and she stumbled forward, almost losing her balance.

Although it was too dark to see, there could be no mistaking the wetness of the water into which she stepped. "Turn on the light, Bobby, turn it on this instant!" She heard rather than saw him clamber up on the laundry hamper to reach the light switch.

A moment later the scene of the flood was illuminated. And flood it was, a slow-motion cascade spilling over the white rounded ledge of the tub—the floor an inch-deep pool, and Bobby as drenched and dripping as any gold-haired merchild ever fished up from the bottom of the ocean. It required but half a minute to turn the spigots off, and less than that to send Bobby posting to the kitchen for a mop.

"Now bring a pail," she ordered, "and when you've brought it, then another mop."

The very first trial, however, proved the mop inadequate. You might as well expect to mop the ocean dry with a pocket handkerchief. Besides, it takes time to wring water out, considerable time and large hands. Already the lake had overflowed the doorsill. In no time at all the whole house would be flooded. In imagination Sally could see the staircase turning into a series of plashing waterfalls, the green-upholstered chairs in the living room floating about and knocking against each other like fence-posts and chicken coops in pictures of the Mississippi when it washes over the levee.

She jerked the towels from the racks to barricade the doorsill. The hall carpet was certainly wet, but not much wetter than before the door was opened. If only there were— Her glance fell on the laundry hamper. Before she could complete her wish for additional towels she had pulled off the lid and overturned the contents on the floor. Bobby had returned, bringing neither pail nor a second mop. He couldn't find them, he announced, which was just as well since they were no longer required.

With an astuteness worthy a child twice his age he grasped at once Sally's plan of battle. Not only did he assist in scattering the sheets and shirts, pajamas and slips and various other oddments widely over the bathroom floor; he stamped valiantly on them with his bare feet to speed the process of absorption. Indeed he was so bent upon making a dry place for Sally to stand that he even sat down upon a pair of paint-streaked overalls and sought to pull himself along the slippery tiles the length of the tub, hand over grubby hand on the rim.

And when, some time later, most of the water had been soaked up, he showed such zeal in throwing the sopping garments into the now empty tub it was only by repeated strict command that Sally succeeded in deterring him from dragging everything out in order to "frow" it all in again.

She surveyed the scene of combat with mixed

feelings, a mild housekeeperly regret for the soggy mass of laundry messing up the clean tub, and honest pride of accomplishment. Except for minor dampnesses here and there, the floor was reasonably dry, the hall carpet was wet no farther than a few feet from the door, and the staircase was intact.

She dispatched Bobby to change into dry clothes (he trotted off obediently, recognizing the quality of command) and sat down on the edge of the hamper to remove her own sopping shoes and stockings before she went to her room to repair her appearance.

Her skirts weren't much wet, but her sleeves were dripping. The elastic band had come off one of her braids, which she succeeded in rebraiding without aid of a comb. Fortunately there was an extra rubber band in her pocket. She would have liked to wash her hands—she didn't see how they could have got so streaked in a clean bathroom; it must have been train dust—but there were no towels. And she mustn't sit down because she'd make a damp spot on the chair.

She was sitting on the rim of the bathtub brushing off the last crumbs of Gran's chicken sandwich, waiting for Bobby to finish with his half, when a voice called from below. "Anybody at home? Bobby? Dorothy? Didn't Sally come? I thought you'd bring her to the store."

It may not have been uneasiness Sally read in Bobby's blue eyes, but it looked very much like it.

He slipped a confiding hand into hers. "You talk to Muvver, Thally," he whispered.

His mother was already at the head of the stairs. "Whatever has been going on here?"

Not until Sally saw the look on her face as she surveyed the contents of the tub did Sally appreciate the magnitude of the damage. For a moment she was afraid she would be held to blame.

"Young man, if I weren't in such a hurry to cook the supper, I'd give you a sound paddling." He retreated behind Sally, clinging to her skirts. "I've a good mind to do it anyhow. How many times have I told you—" She didn't sound really cross, Sally noticed with relief. She sounded like Gran when she was upset or put out because something had gone wrong. "Where's Dorothy?"

"She had to go to rehearsal," Sally explained, adding hastily as she saw Mrs. Brown's expression change, "I made her go. She offered to stay home, but I wouldn't let her. It wouldn't have been fair to the rest of the cast."

"Well, all I can say is it's lucky for us you didn't choose to go with her." She smiled a little. Sally was surprised to see that her eyes were brown, and so was her hair, though not so dark as Sally's.

The danger past, Bobby relinquished his protector's skirts to step boldly into view. "Fido was having a thwim an' the tub wunned over and made a big"—he extended both arms to give a better notion of the size—"big wivver an' it wetted the hall, an' me and Thally dwied it all up."

It must have been difficult to resist his ingratiating smile, but his mother made an effort. "The next time you put Fido into the tub, young man, out he goes, and out to stay," she threatened sternly. Anyone could tell she didn't really mean it. Sally wondered about Fido, but she did not like to ask. He must have run out before Bobby closed the door to keep the water in.

Bobby's mother fetched clean towels to rub his hair dry while Sally washed her face and hands. She would have fetched one of Dorothy's dresses for Sally to change into, but Sally said she had dresses in the suitcase and she'd wait until it came.

Don had already gone to the station, his mother thought. He should be back any minute now. If Sally would excuse her she'd go see about getting supper on the stove. As soon as Sally was ready, if she'd come down to the kitchen they could chat while the supper cooked.

Sally was in the kitchen when Father came home from the store. Absorbed in telling Mrs.

Brown about the Smith's baby and how spry Mrs. Shoup was for an old lady of eighty-three, she did not hear his footsteps. Not until a pair of strong arms seized her from behind, swinging her off the stool where she sat perched, did she realize Father had come.

"It's high time you were home, young lady," he told her. "If you had delayed an hour longer I'd have sent the sheriff to fetch you."

Sally rested her cheek a moment against the sleeve of his overcoat. It smelled of wintry cold and rough tweed and tobacco smoke, a comfortable, satisfying kind of smell. "Aren't you ashamed," she said, "scaring me 'most to bits!"

He planted a kiss on the crown of her brown head. "There now, that'll teach you!" His eyes met hers, blue as Gran's and shining with welcome under their dark brows. She rubbed her cheek against his sleeve a second time. It was odd how she could suddenly feel half homesick for Gran and Westfield at the same time she was so glad to see Father.

Whether it was the success of the rehearsal or something rather like a guilty conscience, her mother's presence or a desire to please her new father, Dorothy was graciously attentive to Sally at the supper table. She insisted upon her taking a larger helping of honey for her hot biscuit, she inquired about her school and whether she liked athletics, and congratulated her on her captaincy.

Don spoke seldom, which did not surprise Sally. None of her friends' big brothers took much notice of people who were still in grade school, even though they were in the upper grades. When she thanked him for bringing the suitcase he said it had been no trouble at all, and said it in such a way she knew it hadn't. His hair and eyes were brown, like his mother's. She was sure she was going to like Don after they got acquainted.

Don carried the empty plates one at a time to the kitchen, and Dorothy brought in the glass dishes of baked custard for dessert. Sally would have volunteered to help except that she still felt strange, although everybody was being especially friendly to her. Maybe if she helped with the dishwashing it would make up for not helping now.

When Dorothy brought Father's dessert she pretended to whisper in his ear, though everyone could plainly hear the words. She needed fifty cents, she told him, needed it awfully. Not for herself, but for something extra-extra special

Daddy didn't happen to have half a dollar he could spare? Her face wore a roguish smile which showed both dimples.

"When you went on an allowance we agreed there were to be no more extras," her mother interposed.

"Now, Mother, please!" Dorothy turned her smile upon her mother. "Just this once! And it's really not for me at all." Her mother made no reply but Sally thought she didn't look pleased. Half a dollar is quite a sum of money.

Father reached into his pocket and laid two quarters on the table. "If a man can't help his daughters out of a tight spot he doesn't deserve to have daughters." His blue eyes crinkled at the corners like Gran's. "What about you, Sally?"

She thought she might need some new schoolbooks on Monday. "We'll manage the books. Isn't there something special you're yearning for too?"

She couldn't think of anything. Besides, she already had some spending money Gran had given her.

"Well, here's a willing taker." Father dropped two bright pennies into Bobby's somewhat sticky, outstretched palms. Bobby held the coins up for display with as much pride as though they were minted gold. "How about it, Don? High school seniors can usually find use for extra cash."

Don replied no, thank you, what Mr. Sampson paid him ought to see him through.

The way Dorothy smiled at Father as she slipped the two quarters into the pocket of her blouse somehow made her seem almost more Father's daughter than Sally was. "He offered me some too," Sally had to remind herself. But something within her argued that he should have done more than offer. He should have insisted. She almost wished she hadn't come to live with Father.

Some time later, when Don had gone upstairs to see that Bobby was still in bed instead of roaming up and down the hall, Father poked his head into the kitchen to inquire what was going on. It sounded like a meeting of the Ladies' Aid, there was so much talking and laughing.

"That's precisely what it is, Frank," he was informed, "three of us aiding each other with the dishwashing. Aren't you sorry you're a man?" Dorothy and Sally both giggled at his gesture of mock regret.

"By the way, Frank," Mrs. Brown continued, "I wish you'd give Bobby a talking-to in the morning. He minds you better than me. He turned the water on again today, and if it hadn't been for Sally the whole house would have been flooded. She arrived just in the nick of time."

"The nick of time"— The words sounded adventurous, like the heroine in a library book. They had a satisfied sound too, as if from now on, things were going to turn out all right. Sally suddenly remembered the shoe box of cookies. "Gran sent you a present, Father. But you'll have to divvy up with the Ladies' Aid, won't he, Dorothy?"

Chapter 3

A Loan

At the breakfast table next morning Mrs. Brown remarked that Dorothy must have got out of bed on the wrong side, she was so hard to please. Sally was inclined to be of the same opinion as she and Dorothy walked together a little later to Sunday school. Or not actually together, for Dorothy managed to keep a step or two in advance. She did not exert herself to talk, answering only in monosyllables when Sally made a remark or asked a question.

Somewhat anxiously Sally reviewed in the privacy of her mind the morning's events, to see whether she might inadvertently have put Dorothy in a bad humor (it makes some people cross if you happen to sit in their special chair or put on their rubbers or gloves by mistake) but she was almost positive she hadn't done anything. She hoped Dorothy wasn't temperamental, like Teresa Walker. It's hard to get on with temperamental persons because they're changeable and you don't know what to expect. Most likely Dorothy had eaten something which disagreed with her, Sally concluded, though it couldn't have been Gran's cookies because no matter how many you had they didn't hurt you.

Dorothy's mood took a decided turn for the better when several of her friends caught up with them. During the exchange of greetings, inquiries after missing companions, complimentary remarks about new hats or scarves or coats—all somewhat subdued because it was Sunday and they were already close upon the church—she gravitated toward the center of the group. Sally found herself standing on the edge, somewhat lost and lonesome until Dorothy should remember to introduce her.

Dorothy was so stylish in her wine-colored coat and hat, she had turned so gay and talkative, it was no wonder the others crowded close around her. The soft way her blond hair curved against her cheek made her even prettier than Sally had imagined from the picture. The thought that as soon as they had time to become better acquainted, Dorothy and she would be just like real sisters kept Sally from feeling completely left out. Any minute now, Dorothy would remember to introduce her.

But just as Dorothy's glance fell upon Sally, a tall gentleman whom the girls addressed as Mr. Bromley stopped to speak to them. He singled out Dorothy and a plump girl named Patsy to inform him about the play. Did they think they'd have it ready for the church bazaar? For he was having the programs printed and wished to make no mistakes in the list of entertainments. Sally followed the group into the Sunday-school room and waited by the door until Dorothy should be free to come for her.

It was a large room, two or three times the size of the one in Westfield, but it wore so familiar an air she might have been there many times before. The light slanting down from the high windows, the Bible scenes framed on the wall, the knots of boys lingering on the farther side as if they hadn't yet made up their minds to remain, their hair sleeked back and their faces scrubbed shiny above their Sunday ties, the animated clusters of girls spreading their coats over the backs of chairs as they took their places—it was all so familiar Sally knew there would be a place for her.

And so there was, a place and a welcome, though not in Dorothy's class. Dorothy explained as she escorted Sally across the room that her friends were older, it would be better for Sally to be with the junior girls, they'd have more in common. Sally swallowed her disappointment and said "Yes, of course" in as natural a tone as she could summon, though she couldn't help thinking a year isn't such a big difference and she was almost as tall as Dorothy right now.

"I've brought you a new pupil, Miss Cole," Dorothy told the teacher. "This is my stepsister, Sally Brown."

It may have been imagination on Sally's part, but Dorothy's manner, or perhaps her intonation of the word, seemed to imply that a stepsister is not really a relative at all—or at best, only a poor relation. Sally was suddenly conscious how far her wrists extended beyond the sleeves of her old coat, and that the coat was shorter than her dress by several inches. Her cheeks turned red. She could feel the red color mounting to her forehead and creeping down her neck.

A pair of gold-rimmed spectacles reflected the beaming glance Miss Cole turned upon Sally. She was a small, comfortable woman with graying hair and a dark silk dress. "We're glad to welcome you, aren't we, girls? Now we're really the Round Dozen! Ellen thought of such a good name for our class," she explained to Sally, "only we haven't been able to use it because we needed one more member. Ellen, suppose you take Sally under your wing for introductions while I go ask Mr. Bromley about our booth for the bazaar."

A thin girl in a plaid dress stepped forward. Sally tried to look pleased to meet her, but when you're a stranger and everybody can see how you've outgrown your coat and knows you're only a stepsister, it is difficult to act natural.

"I saw you yesterday," Ellen said. "I was sitting by the window, and when you went into the house across the street I hoped you'd be in our class." It was like being first choice when the leaders are selecting their teams. Sally's spirits bounded upward.

"If I had known you were there," she told Ellen, "I'd have waved." And after that, though she was still self-conscious, she did not mind the introductions half so much as she thought she would.

The class had adjourned to their own room, the lesson for the day was finished except for the chapter from the Bible (the girls were taking turns with the verses to give everyone a chance) when a boy entered with a note for Miss Cole. Sally didn't think she had ever seen such red hair—not brick red, more nearly coppery. It was curly hair, or would have been if it weren't plastered flat down. Even so, two or three of the drier locks were beginning to spiral upward like corkscrews.

The boy kept one hand buried in his hip pocket, his elbow sticking out at right angles behind him. Sally thought he must have something he was afraid of losing, maybe a self-winding top or a water pistol which he should never have brought to Sunday school—though usually tops and water pistols don't come down from the shelves until spring. While she was speculating from her vantage point at his rear, Miss Cole's lesson leaflet slid to the floor and he stooped to retrieve it.

The hip pocket remained exposed hardly longer than it takes to count five, yet within that brief period so much happened it took Sally several minutes to tell Ellen and Jean about it afterward on the way home. She saw a sharp pinkish nose poke out, a pair of beady eyes blink, and quick as greased lightning a white mouse ran down the boy's trouser leg.

For the fraction of a second the mouse wavered, uncertain whether to seek shelter under Sally's chair or within the folds of Miss Cole's long skirts. The fraction of a second was sufficient to save the day. Letting fall the coin she had brought for the collection, Sally slipped off her chair to kneel on the floor and, under pretext of searching for the nickel, felt around under Miss Cole's skirts until her fingers touched—and closed upon—the errant mouse.

At the very moment she started to rise to her feet, the boy (his name was Max, the two girls informed her, Max Allen) must have missed the mouse, because he dropped down on his knees to look for it. He and Sally bumped heads, but somehow she managed to transfer his property into his keeping before he backed too far away. And all without a single squeak from the mouse or anybody's even suspecting! Max mumbled something, but whether it was an expression of regret for her bumped head or thanks for her assistance, Sally did not know.

As he backed hastily out of the room the class giggled at him and Sally, but she didn't mind. As

a matter of fact she giggled too, though for a different reason. Wouldn't there have been a to-do
if the girls had caught sight of the mouse! Most
girls are scared of mice, even of tame white ones.
Sally was glad she wasn't.

There was roast lamb for dinner, and Sally had a good appetite. Father remarked that perhaps he ought to enroll in Sunday school himself, it seemed to agree so well with Sally. But he was afraid they wouldn't let him sit with the girls. What did Sally think?

She told him gravely that she'd have to ask Miss Cole. Miss Cole might be particular about the kind of company the class kept. But if Father promised to behave himself, maybe Miss Cole would consider it. She would have liked to tell him and the others what had happened, but she didn't wish to get Max into trouble. Ellen and Jean had promised cross their hearts to keep it secret.

Before the cake was served, Don asked please to be excused. Some of the boys were planning to drive to Moorsville and they'd be waiting. His mother thought the roads were too icy to be safe, but he promised they'd drive carefully.

After the dishes were washed and put away, Dorothy had to go to Patsy's house to help make a list of the properties they'd need. They weren't really going to rehearse, she explained to her mother who thought Sunday was not a suitable day for rehearsals, they were just going to list the props and perhaps read over a few of the parts.

Yes, of course she'd take Sally along if Sally wished to go. Honestly, though, she didn't believe Sally would enjoy herself since everyone would be busy and there wouldn't be anything for her to do. Sally said she ought to finish her letter, she'd go with Dorothy another time.

For some reason, however, try as hard as she would, sitting at the new writing table, she could not make the mouse that went to Sunday school sound funny in her description to Gran. She did everything Miss Chapman had taught to make a story interesting: she made some of the sentences short and some long, she put in color words to help Gran picture Max's red hair and blue eyes and green-dotted tie and the pinky-white mouse, but still it didn't sound exciting. She guessed maybe it was because she was used to holding Rufus on her lap when she wrote compositions or a letter. She wondered what he was doing now, and whether Gran was lonesome without her.

She wished she knew Ellen well enough to go over to her house. If she had a book to read she'd sit in the living room where Father was reading the *Atlantic* and Dorothy's mother was looking

through the Sunday papers. But there was nothing
in the bookcase for people of her age, and she
didn't want to ask Mrs. Brown where Dorothy
kept her books. Dorothy might not like lending
them unless she gave permission.

Sally had never known an afternoon to last so
long, not even when she had the mumps and her
neck ached and she had to stay in bed. When
Bobby wakened from a nap she took him for a
walk, and then she helped his mother set plates
and sandwiches on the kitchen table for a cold
snack. Dorothy had returned, and though she
seemed herself to have had a highly satisfactory,
not to say exhilarating, three hours at Patsy's, she
still thought Sally had been wise to stay at home.
It would have been very boring for her because
the girls were older and all they'd talked about
was the props.

Sally had a glass of milk and a sandwich, because sometimes it is easier to pretend an appetite
than to explain why you are not hungry. The cake
she declined, although it was devil's food and she
was fond of chocolate. Mrs. Brown cut a thick
slice to save for Don and one for Sally to take upstairs in case she should be hungry at bedtime.
Notwithstanding Sally's lack of appetite she

couldn't help noticing that Mrs. Brown gave her an extra chunk of fudge icing. She mustn't leave it in the refrigerator, Mrs. Brown warned. The first thing Don always did when he came in from a trip was to raid the icebox. Some day she expected to discover he had devoured even the shelves.

Even at bedtime Sally's appetite had not returned. She managed to dispose of the extra piece of chocolate icing but the cake itself did not tempt her. She wrapped it in a clean handkerchief so it would not dry out. If Gran knew how little she was eating she would be worried. She might even think she was catching a cold or the measles. But she wasn't catching anything. When you're a long way from home and your grandmother is probably packing her clothes right now to go to California and you don't know when you'll ever see her again, you're not interested in food. But if she should happen to be hungry during the night, the cake would be there ready to fall back on.

It was not hunger which awakened Sally in the night, but a noise. At first, before she had fully roused, she thought it was Rufus scratching to be let in. Then she realized it couldn't be, he was still in Westfield. She listened. There it came again,

a muffled, scraping sound. She sat up to hear better. It wasn't upstairs; the upstairs was so quiet
she could almost feel the silence, soft as feathers.

Of course! Why hadn't she thought of it before?
It must be Fido. He must be an outdoor dog; she
hadn't seen him anywhere about. Or maybe it was
Bobby's flood that had been keeping him away.

She had tiptoed halfway down the stairs, her
bathrobe wrapped close around her, when the
thought occurred to her that it might after all not
be Fido. What if it should turn out to be a burglar
trying to get in?

She stopped stock still, holding on to the banister, to consider. It was odd (she had noticed it
more than once on previous occasions) but she
seemed to be two persons at once, each trying to
make her do what it wanted. One kept insisting
that she race back upstairs as fast as she could and
lock her door tight and hide under the bed covers,
not delaying even to cry out a warning to the
household lest the burglar overtake her. The other
self made light of her fear, said there wasn't anything to be afraid of, and even if there was, she
wasn't going to be a cowardy old scare-baby, was
she?

The first self made such a clamor in her mind

it was hard to think, yet underneath she could hear all the while the quiet self holding out to have its own way. The harder she clutched the banister, the more clearly she could think. She reminded herself about the girl in the library book, *Editha's Burglar,* who spoke so persuasively to a burglar that he went away.

But Sally didn't in the least resemble Editha; her hair did not frame a fair face with golden ringlets. Burglars wouldn't be so apt to listen to somebody with straight brown pigtails, or what would be pigtails if they hadn't come undone. Anyhow, she was lots older than Editha, she knew the sensible thing to do in case of burglars is to telephone the police. And most likely it was nothing but Bobby's dog wanting to come in out of the cold.

Slowly, one hand still holding on to the banister, Sally continued her descent, step by measured step. She had reached the last step but one, where the porch light threw a patch of dim yellow into the dark entry hall, when the shadow of a man's head showed itself against the leaded panes of the door. Before there was time to make for the telephone —or for the security of her own bed covers—or even to think whether she was scared or brave, he

lifted his head and the light falling upon it re-
vealed him to be Don.

She took the last two steps in one jump, with
scarcely a false move located the doorknob and
the key in the lock beneath, and a moment later
was greeting him with a muted, shivery "Hello."

"Thanks, Dot," he whispered, pulling off his
overcoat and gloves in the dark and stuffing them
into the blackness of the hall closet. "I was hoping
you'd hear me. I didn't want to wake the whole
house." He tiptoed through the hallway to the
kitchen, holding the swinging door ajar long
enough for Sally to trail in behind him. Almost
simultaneously he reached for the light switch and
opened the refrigerator door.

"I'm not Dorothy." She hoped he wouldn't mind
because she wasn't. "I'm Sally."

He swung around to confront her—a slim figure scarcely shoulder-high, draped in a thick
woolen bathrobe, her dark eyes blinking and shining in the sudden glare of light. "Upon my word,
so you are!" He didn't sound at all displeased, only
astonished. "How in the world did you happen
to hear me?"

"I thought you were Fido," she told him.

"You thought I was *what?*" His voice sounded solemn. She was afraid she had offended him.

"I don't mean I thought you really were Fido." She sought to explain, but it was not easy with his eyes fixed upon her in that odd way. "I didn't want him to have to stay out all night in the cold. Or you either," she added hastily, not wishing to give the impression she was more concerned about a dog than about him.

"Answer me one question, young lady." He might have been a school principal taking a truant to task, he looked so severe. "Have you ever seen this Fido with whom you seem to confuse my honorable person?"

"No," she admitted. "But I've heard Bobby talk about him."

"I suspected as much. Verdict in the defendant's favor!" The pronouncement was weighty, but it didn't make sense. At least it didn't make sense to Sally.

The thought flashed through her mind that perhaps Don was not quite right in his head. Or maybe she was not herself, at least not her ordinary daytime self. Was it possible that in her sleep she had gone Behind the Looking Glass, like Alice?

"Miss Sarah Brown is hereby absolved of intent

to defame, slander, or otherwise belittle the person of the honorable Sir Donald," he continued in the same ponderous manner, bewildering her still further. Then his face broke into a broad grin. "You'd better mind your *p*'s and *q*'s, young lady."

She grinned back at him, half shyly, vastly relieved to discover he was only joking, though she had not the faintest idea what the joke was.

"Bobby's Fido is a frog," he explained. "Not even a real frog, a rubber makeshift, so moth-eaten it's a mortal disgrace to the family." Sally knew that moths don't eat rubber, but she did not correct him. Boys don't know much about housekeeping. He just meant it was so old it was worn out.

"Now do you understand why my feelings were hurt when you implied so close a resemblance between Fido and me you couldn't distinguish one from the other?"

Sally giggled. She liked jokes, but there was about this one a special, grown-up flavor which made it not only a joke but an indirect compliment. When a senior in high school treats you like someone practically his own age you can't help being flattered. She wished she could think of a witty, grown-up remark to make in reply, but she couldn't. A compliment, no matter how agreeable to hear, is always a trifle embarrassing, and when you're embarrassed you can't think fast. But she promised never, never to mix him up with Fido again.

Let her beware of breaking the promise, he warned darkly, because he would not be responsible for the consequences.

He offered to share the chocolate cake, but she would not hear to it. She had a piece upstairs which he'd be doing her a favor to eat. Her haste to fetch it was restricted by the need for stealth. The stairboards showed a marked tendency to creak, which she had not noticed before, and the baluster groaned aloud if she put too much weight against it.

In her own room, the door shut tight to let no ray of light escape, she delayed long enough to rebraid her hair. There wasn't time to make a straight parting down the middle of the front, and both braids turned out somewhat crooked, but at least they didn't look frowsy. Gran always said there was no excuse for frowsiness, no matter how big a hurry you happened to be in. As she surveyed herself in the mirror, Sally couldn't help being glad her bathrobe was new and that it was such a nice bright color. And she was almost sure Don had not noticed her braids had come undone, because he didn't seem to look at her hair, he just looked at her face. Besides, he was mostly looking inside the refrigerator.

By the time she returned with the cake, he had cut several slices of bread and set out the remnants of the roast and a dish of cold peas and what was left of the mint jelly, and was melting butter in a little pan so it would spread easily. They ate their sandwiches standing, leaning against the table for support. It was too much trouble to draw up chairs and seat themselves for so light a repast. Don remarked rather gloomily that if he had known at noon what he knew now, he'd have taken his mother's advice to stay home. As it was, he was completely out of pocket.

"There must have been a big hole in it." Having lost money herself, Sally could sympathize with him. "I hope it wasn't much."

"Every cent I had except two coppers." He plunked them on the table for her to see. "We ran out of gas, and as the other fellows had already squandered their wherewithal on ice cream and candy for their best girls, it was up to me to shell out." Sally wondered whether he had a best girl,

and if he had, whether he hadn't bought her any ice cream and candy, but she didn't like to inquire.

"So now I'm broke. Even if they pay me back, it'll be the end of the week—too late to do me any good so far as getting a birthday present for

Mother is concerned. I get paid myself on Saturday." He poured himself another glass of milk and cut bread and meat for a second sandwich. Sally wasn't halfway through her first one, it was so thick.

She had two dollars he could have, she told him, hesitating a little for fear he might think it wasn't enough. Only when she explained it was some Gran had given her and she had more money besides and there wasn't a single, solitary thing she needed to buy because Father would pay for her schoolbooks, could Don be prevailed upon to accept it. She would have been glad to give it to him, but he would have it only as a loan—to be repaid on Saturday.

Now that it wasn't necessary to rack his brains about how to pay for his mother's birthday present he could cram trig, he told Sally. At first she took trig to be something to eat, but then she realized it must be a subject seniors have to study. He would bring his books to the kitchen. This time of night it was the warmest room in the house.

"Is it hard—trig, I mean?" Sally wanted to know.

"Tough as the hide of a hippopotamus." He cleared a space on the table, piling the dishes in the sink. Sally offered to wash them but he said no, his mother might hear the water running and make him go to bed. Once these exams were over and done with, boy, wouldn't he hit the hay! He'd sleep a solid week.

Although the clock on the shelf was ticking the midnight hour away, Sally was so wide awake herself she didn't see how anybody could possibly be sleepy. She remembered, however, that sometimes in the evening when she had to draw a map showing all the states bordering on their own, or what regions in the United States produced what products, she began to yawn before the clock even struck eight. She told Don she hoped he got a high mark on his examination.

"It'll be mighty hard luck if I don't." He meant it, too, she could tell from his voice. "If I expect to go to college I've got to win a scholarship."

"Father will pay your way," she assured him. "He believes in college. For girls too."

"Your father's not made of money." If Don and she weren't on such good terms with each other she might have thought he was cross with her, but she knew he wasn't. It was only that he was worried. "There's not much profit in a hardware store these days, and it costs a lot to support a family the size of the one your father has taken on. He'll have enough to do to send you and Dot to college. By the time Bob comes along, I'll be on my own and I can see him through."

Sally had never considered how much profit a hardware business might earn. There always seemed to be enough, though of course she and Gran were careful not to waste and Gran often waited for things she needed until there was a sale, to save money.

"Besides, there's no reason why he should be responsible for my college education. He's not my father."

Don was so deeply in earnest, he looked so manly and handsome (she had not noticed before, but there was almost a dimple in his left cheek and he had several tan-colored freckles on his nose), and she longed so much to be of help that obscurely she felt herself taking sides with him. Though there seemed not to be anyone on the other side, against them, still she was on Don's side. If he couldn't go to college, she wouldn't go either.

It may have been her troubled look, or perhaps his own optimism, which prompted him to add in so cheerful a tone she could not but believe him, "Oh, I'll get there, don't you worry. If I don't win a scholarship, I'll work my way through. There are always plenty of odd jobs to be done in college towns."

Sally supposed she had better go to bed, since tomorrow was a school day. She hoped there wasn't much trig to do.

He opened the door for her and held it while she sidled through. "Good night. And thanks for the loan, Sal, old girl."

Long after she had pulled the bed covers up to her chin she kept thinking about Don. Or not so much thinking about him as seeing a picture of him in her mind's eye—and of herself, looking, in her long red bathrobe and red knitted slippers, just like a young lady. Not an ordinary young lady either, but one in a magazine story, to whom the hero confides all his troubles and she helps him out. Even when oncoming drowsiness made the picture blur and grow dim, she could hear in some far, sunny corner of her mind the fading echo of his goodnight, and "Thanks for the loan, Sal, old girl."

If she had a million dollars Don could have it all, every single penny.

Chapter 4

Birthday Presents

Fortunately for Sally, Ellen Gates rang the front doorbell the next morning to take her to school. All during breakfast Sally had been puzzling how to explain to Dorothy's mother without hurting her feelings that she'd rather go by herself. Of course if Dorothy had offered to go with her it would have been different. Dorothy would, she told her mother, only she had promised Mildred and Patsy to help with a poster, and it might make her late.

If a grown person escorts you to school after you are in the upper grades, everybody knows there's a reason. Either you're afraid to stand on your own feet, or you're in trouble, or else you hope your mother can persuade the teacher to promote you although you failed in arithmetic. Sally had no desire to make a bad impression. Once you get a poor reputation it is hard to live it down. Of course Gran attended programs and parent-teacher meetings, but she never had to go to school on Sally's account.

It was a disappointment about Dorothy. Sally tried to tell herself that if they were in the same grade Dorothy would have gone with her, but she didn't really believe it. Maybe it was Mildred and Patsy who didn't want her. They had not acted very friendly when she was introduced. Some girls are snippy unless you're a member of their crowd. But if a girl came to Sally's house to live, she wouldn't go off and leave her. And Sally's friends would give the girl a chance to show what she was like before they made up their minds whether or not to have anything to do with her. In Westfield you enjoyed getting acquainted with new people.

Sally exerted herself to be talkative because she didn't want Ellen to inquire why Dorothy had not waited. It was impossible, however, to keep up a pretense of cheerfulness when the principal assigned her to a different section from Ellen. It would be inadvisable to enroll her in Ellen's section, he explained. Sally had come from a smaller town, and the work here would be more difficult. She must not think she was being demoted.

The half apologetic, half jovial air with which he assured her she would still be in the same grade, only in a less advanced group, was perhaps a concession to Sally's report card. It was a good report card. Or perhaps his horn-rimmed spectacles took note of the discouragement she was attempting to conceal.

"Yes, Mr. Armitage." Sally's voice was creditably steady, and she kept her chin well up.

You don't argue with a principal. Sometimes with a teacher, but not with a principal, no matter how unjust you think his decision is. As they left his office, Ellen looked at Sally, and Sally at Ellen.

"See you at recess, Sally." Ellen slipped her arm through Sally's. She hardly waited until they were out of his hearing to add in an undertone, "Awful old pill!" Her face was red, her voice choked with indignation. "I wish he was in Halifax!"

Sally was too miserable to echo the wish. "Thanks, Ellen." She had to swallow to clear her throat. "See you at recess."

There was a substitute teacher for her section, a Miss Bird who didn't know the name of anybody or which persons were new and which weren't. Sally had a seat toward the back of the room, with boys all around her. The boys had too many things on their minds to pay attention to a girl. It was a relief not to have to act friendly or explain who she was and where she had come from and why she was here.

Sally sat erect, arms crossed on the desk, staring straight in front of her. What would Gran think? Maybe—it was a despairing hope rather than a clear thought—maybe Gran would not let her remain in a school where they put you back without giving you a chance. For no matter what the principal said, being assigned to a slow group is the same as being put back. Maybe Gran would take her to California.

And what would Ruthie say when she heard, and the members of the basketball team, and all her other friends? She didn't see how she could ever hold up her head again. She did hold it up, however, stiffer and stiffer. It may have been to keep the tears from falling, or to hide her humiliation, or perhaps in some wordless part of her mind a resolve had already shaped to hold out in spite of everything until she had won for herself a fair trial. What right had Mr. Armitage to say the

work would be too hard when he hadn't let her try it?

There was a faint whizzing sound, scarcely audible, a rustle of paper, a soft clicking thud. Two missiles had collided above her desk, barely missing her nose as they fell.

Two hands, from opposite directions, reached

simultaneously for the wreckage. In the fraction of a second before it was removed, Sally was able to identify it as two pencil stubs, winged with paper held in place by twisted paper-clips. She was familiar with such gliders in Westfield, though their flights were usually restricted to the playground. Boys who courted trouble in Miss Chapman's room seldom failed to get it. Miss Bird, however, didn't even look around, she was so busy writing a list of words on the board.

Other gliders took to the air in increasing numbers. It might have been field day, with prizes offered. Inevitably, whether by intent or mischance, one of the winged stubs finally overshot itself and landed on Miss Bird's desk. Sally held her breath. To judge from the sudden hush that pervaded the room, she was not the sole uneasy spectator. But Miss Bird was not Miss Chapman, nor even distant kin to her. She finished writing the next word on the blackboard before she turned to announce, "Now let's all copy the spelling words for tomorrow's lesson. Is there anyone who hasn't a pencil?"

Not a hand went up, though Sally noticed that the boys who bent themselves most promptly over their desks were only going through the motions of writing, their fingers quite empty of pencils. The boy on Sally's left bowed his head so low, copied so industriously with the tip of his forefinger upon the empty desk top (he hadn't so much as a scrap of paper) that Sally suspected it must be his pencil and paper resting upon the teacher's desk. She wondered what would happen if Miss Bird should come walking down the aisle to inspect the handwriting as Miss Chapman often did.

Stealthily, her eyes on Miss Bird who stood with her face half turned away toward the window, apparently with nothing to do but wait while the list was copied, Sally slid to the outer edge of her seat. Without a sound she swung both feet into the aisle. Deliberately she lifted first one foot, then the other, setting them down in circumspect succession, very softly at first, with gradually increasing volume of sound, like the approach of rubber-heeled footsteps—*left* right, *left* right, *left* right.

The boy's tow-colored head bowed lower and lower over his empty hand, which still kept up a pretense of writing, zigzagging faster and faster, more and more assiduously as the sound of footsteps became unmistakable. Sally could hardly keep from giggling.

Left right! It was a convincing imitation of rubber-shod heels coming to a sudden halt, a trick Sally and a number of her friends had practiced so diligently they were practically perfect at it. Unfortunately the opportunities to put it to use had been rare, since Miss Chapman was almost never absent from school.

The boy's ears turned red, his writing arm was stricken with paralysis. Head down, he waited for question and reproof.

"Sh-h—sh," Sally whispered. "It's safe now. She's up front." She almost laughed out loud to see his dazed expression as he lifted his head and found the aisle vacant. The joke was too good to keep. She had to share it with him. He grinned with embarrassment, a friendly, wide-mouthed grin that might have grown into a guffaw if Miss Bird had not spoken.

"Has everyone finished copying the list?" Apparently everyone had. Sally had not bothered with it, for the words were all easy ones she had learned way back in fourth or fifth grade—*yesterday, today, tomorrow,* and the like.

At eleven Miss Bird dismissed the class to allow them time to supply themselves with books before the afternoon session. Nobody seemed to have brought any books to study. Indeed, there was so great a dearth of arithmetic and geography and history books, and even of paper that, except for the snow on the windowsills, it might have been the opening day of school in September. The tow-headed boy, whom the others called "Whitey," remarked in an undertone to Sally that Miss Bird needn't expect him to turn up with any books to-day. He had told his little brother to put them away, and it might take a couple of days to locate them. Sally whispered back that if he'd given his brother a penny the books might have been so thoroughly put away Whitey couldn't have found them for a week.

"Wish I'd thought of that!" He grinned appreciatively. "Next time I will."

Though Sally did not mention it to Whitey, she herself intended to waste no time in getting down to work. She meant to get promoted into Ellen's section as soon as possible. And when Father gave her the money to buy books she thought she would ask him for something extra for a birthday present for Don's mother. Her birthday must come soon, else Don would not have had to borrow.

Sally had only the twelve pennies left in her pig bank, since the nickel had gone into the collection at Sunday school. She'd like to buy some·

thing nice for Don's mother, at least a twenty-five cent present. Not only because she was his mother, but because she had given Sally that extra piece of fudge icing and she'd been so pleased that Sally had saved the furniture from being ruined when Bobby turned on the water. Besides, Sally liked her, and when you like someone, you enjoy giving her a present.

When Sally reached the store, Father was busy with a customer who couldn't make up his mind what kind of lock to buy for his garage. Sally lingered at the other end of the room, inspecting the cutlery and coffeepots and curtain rods as though she were a prospective customer. It gave her a slight sense of importance to think all this belonged to Father, with more in the basement besides. Maybe some Saturday when he was short of help he would let her clerk behind the counter. She wished the man with the locks would hurry up, to give her a chance to speak to Father about a birthday gift for Don's mother. She might like one of those green tiles to set a teapot on, or a brass candlestick in case the lights went off.

While Sally was surveying the teakettles a second time, Dorothy came breezing in. She made straight for Father, ignoring the customer except

for a tardy "Excuse me, please," with a hasty
greeting for Sally in passing. Father's smile, the
indulgent gesture with which he replied yes, certainly, put her poster in the front window, he'd be
honored to have it there, and the proprietary air
with which Dorothy pulled open a drawer and
took out a yardstick and some Scotch tape, made

it almost seem that the store belonged to her.

A few minutes later, however, when she asked Sally to be a lamb and climb in among the zinc pails and snow-shovels and rolls of wire in the window to hold the poster while she ran outside to make sure it showed to advantage, it was like being admitted to special partnership. When anyone as attractive and sure of herself as Dorothy requests your assistance, you only wish you could do more for her. You long to do something really hard, to prove your readiness and show your skill and win her gratitude.

A number of boys gathered on the sidewalk to give Dorothy advice, among them Max Allen, whose hair shone copper bright under the brim of his cap. He looked surprised when he saw who was holding the poster. Sally waved, to show she remembered. He waved back, patting his hip pocket with a reminiscent grin. He said something to the other boys, who laughed and looked up at her with such friendly faces she was sure Max must have told them about the mouse.

It was like seeing her name go up on the board when the class ballots were counted. Until she was elected she hadn't dared think how scared she was she might not get any votes. She felt so grateful to people for voting for her, and so happy because they had, she couldn't think of a thing to say except she'd do her best to be a good committee member. That was how Sally felt now—glad and excited and anxious not to disappoint anybody.

There was no opportunity to mention the birthday gift to Father. Other people entered whom he had to serve, since one of the clerks was at lunch and the other was out on repair work. He excused himself from a customer to tell Sally to charge whatever she needed at the bookstore; he would pay for it on the way home. She thought she wouldn't bother him about the present now. She would ask him at suppertime.

Dorothy was curious to know how Sally happened to be acquainted with Max. He was awfully popular, he was older than Sally, he was in Dorothy's class, she said. But he didn't care for girls. Athletes really haven't time for anything except athletics.

"He was at Sunday school." Sally would have explained further, but Dorothy had caught up with Mildred Stone and the two were congratulating each other upon the prominent position their poster of the play occupied.

Sally was almost late for school, it took so long

to extract the twelve pennies from the china bank.
Today was his mother's birthday, Don had whispered to her just before lunch. They always pretended to forget it, in order to surprise her at the
dinner table. If it weren't for Sal's loan, he'd certainly have been stumped for a present.

In the afternoon, as soon as class was dismissed,
Sally hurried to the five-and-ten cent store. It was
not easy to make a selection. The most desirable
things seemed all to come in two's—a pink-rimmed
cup and saucer, ten cents each, salt and pepper
shakers shaped like Dutch children (sold only in
pairs), and a miniature hourglass mounted on a
red stand, a dime for the glass and a dime for the
stand.

She decided upon a tall glass salt shaker for the
kitchen, like the one she had given Gran. Gran
kept it filled with mixed cinnamon and sugar, for
cinnamon toast. It was a great convenience, Gran
often remarked, because it was such a time-saver.
With one of her two remaining pennies Sally
bought a sheet of pink tissue paper to wrap the
gift, and with the other a half yard of pale blue
baby-ribbon to tie it. The birthday card she would
have to make herself, because the printed ones
cost five cents. But if they had cost only one cent

it would have been the same, for she hadn't a single other penny. Anyhow, she liked to draw, and Gran said if love went into the making it was a gift no money could purchase.

She made the drawing on a piece of Aunt Martha's stationery. She would have liked to draw a gas stove with cinnamon toast coming hot out of the oven and a black kitten sniffing and miaowing to show how good it smelled, or else a ring of kittens dancing around a tall cinnamon and sugar shaker. But it takes time to sketch soft fur and perky ears and a saucy expression for even one kitten, and there wasn't much time. She hoped Don's mother would like a picture of a birthday cake almost as well, with the flames wreathing up from the candles to spell HAPPY BIRTHDAY.

What to write on the envelope posed a problem. "Mrs. Brown" did not seem very friendly, especially since she was Father's wife and treated Sally just like one of the family. But she didn't believe Dorothy would think she had a right to call her "Mother." Whenever Dorothy mentioned her to Sally she always spoke of her as "my mother." Don would not mind Sally's writing the word on the envelope, she was certain. From the way he said "Mother" or "Mom" he seemed to think she belonged as much to the others as to him. But of course she wasn't really related to Sally except by marriage, and Dorothy had a rightful claim to her. Probably it would be better not to call her anything, not to hurt anybody's feelings.

In square letters, embellished at intervals with decorative curlicues, Sally printed MANY HAPPY RETURNS OF THE DAY on the envelope, and slipped it underneath the pale blue bowknot on the pink-wrapped package.

It was a gay dinner. Though everyone was careful not to mention birthdays, in order to keep the surprise till the end, there were so many jokes told, so much laughing, so many sly nods and secret side glances, and such a general air of festivity Sally thought even if she had not known, she would have guessed it was somebody's anniversary.

Mrs. Brown, however, seemed not to suspect a thing. She must have forgotten what day it was. Grown persons often do, though they remember other people's birthdays. It was comical to see how blank she looked when Bobby unexpectedly lifted his treble with an "I'se dot a pwesent for—"

Don shook his head in warning. "Look at your hands, Bobby, you've got jelly on them," Dorothy interrupted the three-year-old. "Let's go wash them."

There was vanilla ice cream for dessert, which Father had "happened to want" as he passed the drugstore on his way home. While Mrs. Brown and Sally were serving it in the pantry, Don and Dorothy brought out the gifts. Sally carried in the last of the dessert dishes in time to join the family in singing *Happy Birthday to You.*

"Supwise—ice cweam—ice cweam!" chanted Bobby in shrill treble, with major stress upon the more substantial pleasure.

"A party! And presents!" Mrs. Brown raised her hands in astonishment. "It must be a birthday!" A chorus of voices assured her it was indeed.

She opened Bobby's gift first, a checkered potholder, red and blue. Between tastes of frozen cream that young gentleman acknowledged the gift and submitted to a kiss in payment. The box of candy, decorated with a wide pink satin bow, was of Don's giving. His mother insisted that the others sample the chocolates while she opened the next package. A moment later she held up for admiration a pair of salt and pepper shakers, painted with forget-me-nots, far more elegant than anything the five-and-ten cent store had to offer.

The bonbon Sally was nibbling quite lost its savor. It might have been a wad of cotton instead of perfume-flavored candy out of a fancy box. Her own present was so plain, compared to Dorothy's, so cheap and kitcheny-looking, she wished she could hide before anyone saw it. She was ashamed to think how poor a gift it was. If only she didn't have to remain in the room while Dorothy's mother untied it! Everyone would look first at the shaker and then at Sally, and feel sorry for her because what she had given wasn't any better.

"Where did this come from? You, Frank?" Mrs. Brown inquired around the table. "Dorothy? Don?"

Sally's face burned, her throat was dry as dust. She tried to summon voice to claim the homely article.

"Because ever since we moved into this house it's precisely what I have needed! A salt shaker that doesn't have to be filled every few minutes, just when I'm in the biggest hurry! Someone must be psychic, to look into my mind and read my wish."

Sally did not know what *psychic* meant, but from the way Dorothy's mother smiled (she almost had a dimple in her cheek, like Don) it must be a compliment. And she honestly seemed to appreciate the shaker every bit as much as the other things, maybe even a tiny bit more.

"There's a birthday card that goes with it," Sally reminded her. The words came out somewhat breathless, because to bounce all the way up from dejectedness to joy in less than a minute is almost dizzying.

"You didn't make this yourself, Sally? But certainly you must have!" Mrs. Brown answered her own question. "None of the others can draw a straight line. Look, children, we have a real artist in the family." Don declared it had quite a professional touch, and even Dorothy praised it. Sally felt herself blushing, but she was too happy to care how red her cheeks turned.

Father held the birthday card to his nose. "Angel food!" he announced. "I can tell by the smell. I'm tempted to eat it."

"Father!" Sally affected to be shocked. "You mustn't sniff your food, Father Brown, it's not polite. And think what a bad exampie for your children!" A giggle flickered through the mock reproof, light as candle flame.

"Me too," begged Bobby with a gleeful wave of his spoon. "Me wants to smiff too, Thally!"

Chapter 5

A Valentine

It was not until the following week the family learned that Sally had been assigned to a slow group. Many times she longed for the steadying support of their sympathy, but everyone seemed to take it for granted she was happy at school and no one made inquiries. Nor did there ever seem to be an opportune time to bring up the subject herself.

At table the conversation touched chiefly upon lighter matters, incidents of the day's housekeeping, the weather, customers (a little boy had brought an empty glass jar for three pennies' worth of red-and-green striped paint for his dog kennel), news of the neighbors, the progress of Dorothy's play. Mrs. Brown and Father and Dorothy did most of the talking, though now and then Sally or Don joined in, or Bobby contributed a remark about Fido or the garage with a big tin roof he was building in the basement.

"So that's where my kitchen tray went!" protested his mother. "I have hunted it high and low. It's aluminum, Cousin Kate gave it to me for Christmas, and I can't get along without it," adding soothingly as Bobby's face began to pucker ominously, "Your father will bring you a shiny new piece of tin for a roof."

"Better than that," promised Father. "I'll save the scraps from the new furnace pipe we're making. Master Bob can build an entire garage of the pieces."

Dorothy came down to breakfast later than usual this morning. She was wearing her best dress, of soft green wool. She was invited to a party after school, she informed the table, addressing herself rather more to Father than anyone else. Would she pass muster?

Don, who was used to her little vanities, remarked with a grin that she might get by, she certainly ought to, to repay her for all the time spent at the mirror. Her mother told her to eat her cereal before it got cold, but Father insisted that she turn around for inspection. The soft green color was so becoming, her long lashes rested so demurely against her cheeks as she waited for his judgment, Sally was anxious lest Father might fall short in his praise. Gran said he wasn't very observant.

"If prizes are awarded," he asserted, "daughter Dorothy will carry off all the firsts."

Dorothy's mother inquired how Sally liked Miss Johnson. "She teaches the other section," Sally explained. "Miss Clancey is the teacher for my room, only she broke her arm. We have a substitute."

She hoped the mention of Miss Clancey's name would be a cue for further questioning. She didn't think she could continue much longer pretending she was happy at school. Even Whitey wished openly for Miss Clancey, although she would put up with no nonsense and was a stickler for homework. It may be fun for a day or two to discomfit and out-maneuver an ineffectual teacher, but after a while doing as you please loses its novelty and you'd welcome the return of orderly rule.

Miss Bird had still learned hardly any of their names, and no matter how impudent or disobedient anyone might be, she pretended he hadn't been.

She was what Gran called "blind in her mind's eye." That was the way Mrs. Walker acted about Teresa, as if by shutting her eyes to Teresa's insolence she made it not exist. Sally couldn't understand why a grown-up person like Mrs. Walker or Miss Bird didn't know better.

"Miss Clancey!" exclaimed Dorothy. "Are you in her room?" There was a perceptible tinge of something akin to scorn in her manner. Sally nodded uncomfortably. "Why, Miss Clancey teaches the dumb-bells."

"I wouldn't say that," interposed Dorothy's mother. "Some of the children are special cases. Everybody knows that Sally gets good marks in school."

Sally swallowed. Her face felt burning hot and there was a hard lump in her throat which made it almost impossible for words to come through. "Mr. Armitage said I had come from a smaller school." The explanation was inadequate, she knew, but that was what he had said.

"Maybe I should speak to him," suggested Mrs. Brown. "Wouldn't you like me to go to school with you tomorrow? I think I could persuade him."

"Oh, no, thank you." Sally hurriedly declined

the proffered aid, and declined it the more earnestly because she was so greatly tempted. "It'll be all right after Miss Clancey comes back to make the boys behave."

"The principal must know best," Father remarked. He was helping Bobby butter his toast. "Westfield is only a village. It's reasonable to suppose that the Westfield school is less advanced than ours." He didn't want Sally to feel she was to blame.

But Sally did not understand. She had counted on Father as she counted on Gran. His quiet dismissal of the matter as of little importance, his seeming failure to sympathize with her or to stand up for her, left her for a moment defenseless. She felt shut out, forsaken. The lump thickened in her throat, her eyes smarted with scalding tears she could scarcely keep blinked back.

Then pride came to her rescue. Not only had Father not expressed any confidence in her ability, he was willing to let the others believe she belonged in a retarded group. She would get herself promoted out of Miss Clancey's room just to show him. She wouldn't let anybody help her, and particularly not Father.

If it had been Dorothy he would have gone

straight to the principal to set things right. He treated Dorothy more like his own daughter than Sally. Well, let him! If that was how he felt about Sally, she would feel the same way about him. She would go back to Westfield to live with Gran. But before she went she would prove that she didn't belong with the dumb-bells any more than Dorothy did. It was Father who was to blame, it wasn't Dorothy, she told herself, unwilling even in her rankling hurt to admit an imperfection there.

Mrs. Brown excused herself to give directions to the washerwoman, who had appeared earlier than she was expected. Father turned to Don. "We ought soon select a college for you, to get your application in before it's too late. Have you thought about the state university?"

Don said he had thought about the university, but he wasn't sure he would go to college. He might go to work. Mr. Sampson had offered him a full-time position as soon as school closed.

"Not go to college?" Father frowned. "Every young person needs a college education these days, to make the most of himself. Surely you're not planning to spend your life working for Mr. Sampson?"

Don flushed. "No, sir," he replied in a low voice.

"I'd expect to get something better after a year or two." From the way he looked, Sally could tell that his feelings were hurt.

"I am disappointed that you don't care to continue your education, Don."

To Sally's ears, and perhaps to Don's, Father's statement sounded like a rebuke. What right had Father to say Don didn't want to go to college? Of course Don wanted to go. The only reason he didn't tell Father was because he didn't wish to be an expense. Don was proud. That was why he studied late at night, to win a scholarship so it wouldn't cost Father anything. It was not fair of Father to find fault with him. Somebody ought to tell Father so too, but she supposed nobody would. Anyhow he ought to know without being told, because he was a grown-up man with hair beginning to turn gray at the temples. He had no right to talk like that to Don when he didn't know anything about it.

Sally ranged herself solidly behind Don. Every penny she could save, she'd give to Don to help pay his way through college. If she were he, she wouldn't take any of Father's money either; she'd pay her own way. And if Don didn't go to college, she wouldn't go either. In the warm rush of sym-

pathy for Don, her eagerness to aid him, she forgot how indifferently Father had seemed to pass
over her own unspoken need for understanding.
Or if she did not entirely forget, it no longer
seemed important.

She and Don walked part way to school together.
Neither talked much, but their silence was companionable. At the corner where he must turn off,
three or four of his friends were waiting. "Fellows, I want you to meet my best girl, Sally Brown
—Tom Adams, Pete Hopkinson, Skids Cassidy,
and Shorty Stover." They shook hands with her
as politely as though she too were a senior in high
school.

"Let me warn you fellows"—and though Don's
tone was bantering, Sally was pretty sure he meant
it—"you're not to cut in on my best gal Sal without
my permission!"

Skids Cassidy winked at her, and she giggled.
She might have winked back, but it's hard to wink
when you are laughing. The icy pavement along
which she alternately ran and slid the long block
to school might have been a primrose lane in Para-
dise, the wind was whistling so spring-like a song
in her ears.

After arithmetic class, Miss Bird sent two of the boys to the grocery store for a cardboard carton to use for a valentine box. Sally had noticed that Miss Bird always picked out the most troublesome boys to go on errands. It didn't seem just that they should have the privilege, it ought to be a reward for good behavior, but many of the things Miss Bird did were not fair. She never scolded anybody except girls. Nor did she scold the girls if they had especially nice clothes or were bold enough to talk back, like Angelina Tubbs.

Angelina was the oldest girl in the class, and the biggest. She had a permanent wave and a ring she boasted was a real diamond which she was continually rubbing against her skirt to make it shine. But it didn't sparkle at all, and Sally believed it must be only an imitation diamond, or maybe just plain glass. Angelina wore a different dress to school almost every day, some with fancy trimmings, but the dresses weren't always clean. Although she went out of her way to be friendly to Sally, even offering to let her wear the diamond ring, Sally did not like her. You can't really like anybody who says flattering things to people's faces and then turns right around and talks about them behind their backs. Sally was relieved that it was Adelaide and Jessie Miss Bird appointed to help Angelina decorate the valentine box, and not her.

If she had been in Westfield it would have been

impossible to forget that today was the fourteenth
of February. She and Ruthie would have been
buying valentines and collecting pennies from the
class for a flowery big one to surprise Miss Chapman, and Gran would be baking crisp heart-
shaped cookies sprinkled with pink sugar, and
somebody would be giving a party after school. It
must be a valentine party Dorothy was invited to.

It didn't matter that it was St. Valentine's day,
Sally tried to convince herself. She was not good
enough friends with people in the room to exchange valentines with them, except Jim Sands
and Whitey and a few of the other boys, and you
don't give valentines to boys. What worried her,
however, was that it would be dreadfully humili-
ating to be the only person whose name wasn't
called to come up front to receive a valentine. The
more she thought about it, the greater ignominy
it seemed. It was mortifying to contemplate in
imagination how Angelina would whisper about
her behind her back. Angelina didn't like it because at recess Sally always played with Ellen and
Jean and their friends instead of with her.

If she hurried through lunch there would be
time to buy a valentine at the drugstore to send
herself. But a drugstore valentine would almost

certainly cost five cents. It would be a shame to waste a whole nickel when she needed to save every penny for Don. She would have to make herself one. If she put it inside one of Aunt Martha's envelopes nobody would see that it was homemade.

During study hour, screened behind her geography book, Sally labored at the valentine. It was a picture of herself standing beside a train (only one end of the car showed, because there wasn't space on the paper for more) pocketbook in hand, a bulging suitcase at her feet, two short braids sticking out from under her hat. It was a side view, for she was better at drawing profiles than fronts of faces. As the sketch grew under her fingers, it became more and more lifelike—the details exaggerated sufficiently to make it a comic valentine but not an ugly one—the quill in her hat at a rakish angle, her nose slightly uptilted with a suggestion of freckles, her old coat a size or two smaller than it actually was. She was so pleased with her own handiwork she could hardly refrain from showing it to Whitey, to hear him praise it. But she mustn't; she must keep it secret. She might show it to Don when she got home.

The time assigned to practice penmanship she

spent composing verses to accompany the drawing. The first three lines came easily, just from looking **at** the picture:

> *Miss Sally Brown*
> *Has come to town,*
> *In pigtails.*

After that, it was a struggle. None of the other words that rhymed with *Brown* fitted in very well —*clown, crown, down, frown, noun.* She tried them all, finally settling upon *frown* as the most promising.

> *Now don't you frown*
> *At Sally Brown*
> *'S pigtails.*

> *For if you do,*
> *I tell you true,*
> *There'll be loud wails.*

The last line was too long and bumpy, but if **a** single word was omitted it didn't make sense. Anyhow the verses rhymed, and the oftener she reread them the more satisfactory they sounded. During spelling lesson she finished printing the lines of the jingle underneath the picture.

The afternoon history class was so noisy Miss

Bird threatened not to let them have a valentine box, a possibility which, though nobody believed she would carry out the threat, it was not quite safe to ignore. Even then the boys kept scuffling their feet back and forth under their desks, looking up at her innocently all the while or replying with an air of pained virtue, when she charged any of them with misbehavior, "Who, me?"

It was useless to study your lessons for Miss Bird. Frequently she didn't know the answers herself. She had to keep her book open where she could see what it said. Often the boys, and girls too, for that matter, asked questions they had gleaned from older brothers and sisters to trip her. But Miss Bird would never admit she didn't know. She would smile a superior little smile and advise them to look it up themselves, so they would be sure to remember. Which of course fooled nobody.

Whitey could mimic her smile, her prim voice, the fluttering movement of the two last fingers on her left hand with its bright new engagement ring with such consummate skill you were almost persuaded he had actually turned into Miss Bird.

At first Sally used to feel sorry for her because she was having such a hard time and everyone took advantage of her. But you can't go on forever feeling sorry for a person like Miss Bird who never makes any effort to help herself. If she would see to it that the classes got down to work and behaved themselves, they wouldn't take advantage of her. If only Miss Clancey would return, to make it possible to study and get promoted into Ellen's section!

The threat about the valentine box was wearing thin, the disorder was increasing. Miss Bird had her head tilted sideward, squinting at the open page of her book (pretending she was looking for a pencil) to see whether Jessie had answered correctly about the Monroe Doctrine. The door opened and a small, reddish-haired woman entered, her arm in a plaster cast. For a moment there was complete silence in the room. Then almost as one person the class surged forward to greet her.

"Miss Clancey! Miss Clancey! Have you come to stay? Are you all right, Miss Clancey?"

Sally remained in the background because she was not acquainted. No one, however, shouted "Hurrah!" with livelier cheer than she when Miss Clancey promised to teach them next week. This afternoon she was only a visitor.

Miss Bird hastily dismissed the history class and gave Miss Clancey the chair behind the desk because it was the most comfortable. Her directions to the class to put away their books and tidy up their desks and pick up the scraps of paper from the floor were complied with almost before they were spoken. Sally wondered whether Miss Clancey supposed they always obeyed Miss Bird as well as this. It would have been embarrassing for Miss Bird if they acted the way they usually did. Sally was relieved that they were behaving themselves. Now that Miss Bird was not to be their teacher any longer, Sally was beginning to feel sorry for her again.

Adelaide and Jim read off the names on the valentines, handing them out one at a time from the crepe-paper trimmed box. Most of the girls had already received two or three, and a number of the boys more than one (funny ones, to judge from their expressions) before Sally's name was called. She had begun to worry lest hers had got lost, it took so long to appear.

She marched up to the front of the room wearing as surprised and pleased an expression as she could assume, to keep anyone from suspecting whose hand it was that had printed SALLY BROWN

in careful block letters on the envelope. One valen-ine isn't very many, but it's enough to keep people from remarking behind your back that you didn't get any.

After the box had been emptied, someone pro-posed that they each give Miss Clancey their pret-tiest valentine because if they had known she was coming they would have sent her some. But she wouldn't let them. Her conscience would be up in arms, she declared, if she permitted them to rob themselves. Which, together with her comfortable, half teasing smile, made them all the more eager to shower her with their best. In the end it was decided that everybody should place one valentine on the ledge of the blackboard for her to make her choice.

As Sally slipped her homemade one in among the funny ones the boys had lined up at the farther end of the ledge, she couldn't help regretting it was not a store-bought satin heart with painted flowers and twining bowknots for Miss Clancey's pleasure, no matter how dear it cost. For a teacher as nice as Miss Clancey, ten or fifteen cents wouldn't be a bit too much to spend.

Deliberately, from end to end of the row and then back again, Miss Clancey surveyed the offerings, not scanting a single one. Sally knew which she would take if she were choosing (the one with cut-out figures of a little boy and girl, with tiny real feathers on their hats, the boy's red, the girl's yellow), but Miss Clancey lingered over the penny valentines and the boys' comics rather than the expensive ones. Sally guessed maybe that was why the boys liked her—she enjoyed jokes.

Miss Bird's brown sleeve cut off Sally's view when the choice was finally made, though she could see that it was from the side where the funny pictures were. From the subdued exclamations at the front of the room she could tell that people were surprised. She herself was a little disappointed that it had not been the one with feathers. But the disappointment lasted less than a moment, for when Miss Clancey held the valentine up for the class to view, it was Sally's homemade one.

Sally was so astonished she could hardly find breath to speak up when Miss Clancey announced that if the owner was willing, she would keep this valentine for herself.

"Yes, Miss Clancey," she bobbed out of her seat to assure her, sliding hastily back down into it as everybody turned to gaze at her. She was embarrassed, realizing that she must not have sounded very polite. She should have said she'd be pleased to have Miss Clancey keep it, or she was more than welcome, or something mannerly like that.

"Perhaps you wonder why I selected this particular valentine." Everyone faced forward again to listen to Miss Clancey. "It was difficult to make a choice, I must admit, because I was tempted to choose them all. Two reasons prompted my choice. One reason is that the valentine is handmade, and handmade things have individuality."

Sally drew a long breath. *Individuality*—nobody had ever said that about her work before. It made her want to try her level best, not only in drawing but in everything else.

"The second reason, and I'm sure you all agree with me"—Miss Clancey held up the sketch again so the class could have a second look—"is that it's such a jolly picture it makes me feel cheerful to look at it."

The class nodded approvingly, and some smiled and some turned to look at Sally and others clapped. Honestly, Sally thought to herself, blushing with pride and pleasure, honestly and truly it was such a friendly class she wouldn't mind if she didn't get promoted out of it, so long as Miss Clancey was going to be their teacher.

A few minutes later, Angelina took occasion to pass by Sally's desk. "I bet you sent that valentine to yourself," she whispered, not without malice.

"Who, me?" The wide-eyed innocence with which Sally looked up at her would have done credit to Whitey.

Angelina scowled.

Chapter 6

An Escape

It had been a dismal night. For a long time Sally had lain awake, alternating between righteous indignation and despair, twisting and turning and flopping from side to side until the bed was rough with wrinkles. When at last she fell asleep, sleep brought no comfort. In her dreams Dorothy's remarks took on a nightmarish quality, and the coolness with which Dorothy had criticized her hardened into stone.

Sally had been coming down the stairs with her arithmetic book, when she overheard Dorothy. "Before you go into the living room, Dorothy," her mother had said, "I want you to promise to invite Sally to go with you and Mildred to the motion picture tomorrow afternoon after school."

"Oh, Mother, why do I have to?" Sally heard the swish of the dishtowel as Dorothy flapped it petulantly against the sink. "Mildred and Patsy won't want her tagging along."

"Let them go by themselves then. I've never had a very high opinion of Mildred Stone, and I'd be pleased to have you see less of her. Sally is your sister."

"Now, really, Mother, you know she's not really. A stepsister's not the same, and you know it. She's so old-fashioned, with those pigtails and all. And that coat of hers— She looks positively countrified, it's so antiquated. People will think we are poverty-stricken." Dorothy's voice was half pleading, half pettish. "Even her name is old-fashioned."

"She has a good name. *Sarah* is a Bible name. And I like her braids. When I was a girl everybody wore braids." There was a heartiness in Mrs. Brown's manner of speaking which warmed Sally's pulse and made it possible to breathe again. "As for the coat, if you're too snobbish to be seen in company with a shabby coat, you're no daughter of mine. It must be Mildred who is responsible for such cheap, ill-bred notions. I thought you had more character, Dorothy."

In the silence which followed, Sally thought she could hear Dorothy sniffling, as though her feelings had been hurt. She hoped they were; they deserved to be.

"I have thought of getting her a new coat," Mrs. Brown continued, "but I was afraid she might take it as disparaging her grandmother's judgment. Her grandmother must have thought the coat would last the winter through. And it isn't long now until spring." There was another silence. Then, "I'm waiting, Dorothy," her mother reminded her.

Dorothy's reply was slow in coming, and when it came, was so lacking in conviction Sally's last hope crumbled. If Dorothy had sounded as though she'd really like to invite Sally, now that her mother had pointed out how inconsiderate it is to judge people by the clothes they wear, Sally would have forgiven her.

Since before Christmas she had cherished in imagination an ideal Dorothy, and though the real one had occasionally proved less friendly and companionable than the ideal, Sally had been unwilling to admit it. Slights which could not be ignored, she made excuse for. When you long with all your heart to be friends with someone, especially someone who can be as winsome as Dorothy, who part of the time treats you as though she too wishes to be friends, you can't help trying not to see her faults.

"I'll invite her, Mother." So clearly implied in Dorothy's tone was an "I hope she won't accept," Sally almost fancied she heard the echo of the words.

Disappointment, hurt pride, resentment smoldered into flame, making such a hotness in Sally's chest her throat and eyes smarted. But not with tears. There were no tears until much later, after she had gone to bed, and then only a few as she remembered how far away California was and how short a ride two dollars would pay for on the train. Had it been summer, she would have gone home, to Westfield, though she had to walk every step of the way. But it was winter, and Gran was visiting Aunt Martha. When you reach Sally's age you realize it would be foolish to run away unless there is someone to take you in, especially in wintertime.

But if Dorothy thought Sally would cut her pigtails on her account, she was mightily mistaken. Sally and Ruth had been letting their hair grow since early last summer. They both wished to have braids. They had bet each other a pineapple ice cream soda whose braids would grow longer. Sally would be willing, however, to go part way to please Dorothy. She and Gran both believed it was better to co-operate with people, even when you'd rather not.

Tossing the covers heavily back, she climbed out of bed, closed the door to keep the light from shining out, and rummaged in the drawer for the curlers she had used for the Christmas pageant. She was tired, she was beginning to yawn, her hands and feet were cold, but lock by separate lock she wound all her front hair around the thin wire strips. She rolled it tight to keep it from coming undone, and then, doubly to insure success, padded down the hall to the bathroom, to stand on the chill floor tiles first on one icy foot, then the other, while she dampened the curls. It was a tedious process, because it was not safe to turn the water on more than a trickle lest it waken somebody up.

Shivering, she crawled back into bed, to fall into a troubled sleep in which Dorothy, in the likeness of a witch, was seeking to put a spell upon her to change her into stone so people could say things about her behind her back. The spell made her head ache as though sharp pebbles were pressing into her temple. Half rousing, she fumbled with some of the offending curlers until they were loosened. Then she slept again, uneasily.

She wakened early, as tired as though she had not slept. The dreary sense of having been rejected by Dorothy wakened with her. She wished she had never come to Doncaster, she wished she were back in Westfield with people who liked her, she wished she were dead.

She dressed hastily, hoping to finish breakfast before Dorothy appeared. Not until she caught sight of herself in the bathroom mirror as she dried her face did she remember the curlers. One side of her hair hung straight, the other was plucked back from her forehead in a series of knobby lumps. Well, she had made an effort to meet Dorothy halfway about her hair, she told herself moodily; it wasn't her fault it didn't turn out the way it should. In the back of her mind she almost felt it was Dorothy's fault. She would brush out the curl and wear her braids as usual, whatever remarks Dorothy might choose to make about them.

Brush as she would, however, the curl remained. Indeed, the harder she brushed, the fuzzier her hair became. On one side, that is. It stood up like a dark bush, obstinate as Sally herself when her temper was aroused. As much of it as she could, she restrained in an uneven plait, but even while she was twisting a rubber band around the end, wisps were escaping. The conviction that Dorothy was to blame grew upon her. If Dorothy hadn't talked about her, this wouldn't have happened. Just wait, she'd get even with her. She'd show her she could give as good as she got. A stepsister— that's what Dorothy was, a snippy old stepsister.

It was so early when Sally went down to breakfast only Father and Don were at the table. Bobby seemed to be catching a cold, Father told Sally, looking up from his newspaper to say good-morning; his mother was up in his room.

Father did not approve of reading at the table, he said it was a bad habit, but he was always so busy at the store there was no other opportunity to find out what was happening in the world. Sally liked to read a book while she ate her toast, and sometimes Gran let her. She wished she had a book now. If Father could read at the table, why shouldn't she?

Don, who was surreptitiously working a trigo-

nometry problem on his lap, gave her a friendly nod and shoved the bowl of oranges within her reach. They ate in silence until Father departed, by which time Don's problem had found a solution. "How's everything this morning?" he inquired, helping himself liberally to the blackberry jam.

It was a cue for conversation. Sally met his question with one of her own. "Do I look different, Don?" She waited anxiously for his verdict.

He glanced up from the jam pot. "You seem to

have the customary number of eyes, ears, nose, *et cetera*. Yes, I'd recognize you anywhere."

"Seriously, Don, I mean it. It's my hair." If he didn't notice anything different after his attention was called to it, it would be safe to appear at school.

He gave her a longer look, noting perhaps the anxiety in her eyes. "Well, just possibly you appear a little Jekyll-ish and Hyde-ish this morning." He might have been a doctor remarking that her temperature was up a trifle, barely above normal, nothing to worry about.

She did not know what the words meant. "Dr. Jekyll and Mr. Hyde? They were two men who lived together inside the same body," he explained.

Sally turned the explanation over in her mind. "I don't see how they could," she questioned. "Where'd they have room for so many arms and legs? And how could they walk without getting into each other's way?"

"Oh, they got into each other's way. You're one hundred per cent correct on that score." The almost dimple in his cheek made her think of his mother and how much alike he and she were, treating her just as if she belonged.

"As a matter of fact, they were only one man,

except figuratively. When he was good he was Dr. Jekyll, and when he was bad he was Mr. Hyde. Two sides to his character, you understand. Like the mornings you get out of bed on the wrong side, and get into trouble all day. Or maybe you never get up on the wrong side," he added teasingly.

Sally was beginning to feel considerably less forlorn, as though the world might after all prove to be not entirely flat and stale. "I did this morning," she confessed.

"Let me recommend a cup of coffee, Sal. There's nothing so potent to brace your fighting arm as a stiff drink of coffee." He was still teasing, but he was solicitous too. "What about it, old girl?"

His brotherly "old girl" decided her. Gran said coffee was not good for growing children, and Sally disliked the taste of it, but she nodded her willingness to undergo the remedy. He poured himself a second cup to keep her company. By dint of determination and the addition of generous quantities of sugar and cream she succeeded in downing the scalding liquid to the last drop.

"How do you feel now?" Don wished to know. "Ready to give the Old Nick the slip?"

The taste of coffee was still too unpalatably

recent for her to know how she felt, except that there was a hot streak inside where the drink had gone down. "I feel better," she said, too loyal to disappoint him.

Strangely, or perhaps not strangely after all, no sooner had she said so than she began actually to feel better. It may have been the heat of the beverage, it may have been the warmth that comes of being understood and befriended, but something was generating a glow within her. She did not linger at the table, having no desire to see Dorothy. Besides, she had promised to correct spelling papers for Miss Clancey. By the time she reached the school building she felt quite cheerful, notwithstanding the bleak wind and lowering sky.

It was not an ordinary kind of cheerfulness, however. It resembled recklessness more than good humor, it was exhilarating rather than comfortable. If she was a stepsister (and Dorothy would not let her be anything else) she'd act like a stepsister. She was tired of behaving herself and wearing a seedy old coat and having Dorothy go off and leave her. If Dorothy could act bad-tempered, so could she.

And if she got into trouble it would be Dorothy's fault. Moreover, it would be Dorothy who would feel disgraced when everybody heard about it. Sally didn't care what anybody said about her, behind her back or to her face. She'd show them she could give as good as she got. Just let them try!

It wasn't yet eight o'clock, the janitor objected when after prolonged banging at the back door she brought him grumbling to see who was there. It was against the rules to admit her for another half hour; he wasn't going to break the rules for nobody, he wasn't, and that was that!

But that wasn't that, he soon discovered, for Sally overrode his objections with pleas not to make Miss Clancey do the spelling papers, poor Miss Clancey with her broken arm in a plaster cast who probably ought not be coming to school at all.

The smiling "Thank you, Mr. Namm, I'm sure Miss Clancey will appreciate it," with which Sally rewarded his grudging turn of the lock may not have been altogether free of personal triumph. Since Mr. Namm was re-locking the door against other intruders, perhaps he failed to observe the quality of the smile.

Emboldened by her initial success, Sally hung her hat and coat on the hook Angelina had appropriated as her special property. Lest Angelina might think it had been done inadvertently, she pinned a sheet of paper to the coat with a legend "DO NOT DISTURB. S. B." in large print.

She corrected Angelina's paper first of all. There being no misspellings, it was necessary to mark it *100,* but she made the figure microscopically small and followed it with a giant interrogation mark. Angelina would know what that meant. It meant that Sally knew she copied the hard words. The other papers were of no particular interest, though she derived a mild satisfaction from drawing extra large checks against the errors of the two or three people she did not like.

The papers completed, she looked around for something else to do. Her desk needed tidying, but she was in no mood to be concerned about her own shortcomings. She straightened out Whitey's books and hid his pencil under his ruler, to give him a reason to borrow from Jim. Whenever possible, Jim and Whitey borrowed because it gave them a chance to talk to each other. There was little other opportunity for conversation under Miss Clancey's watchful eye.

Nor were Adelaide and Jessie, Angelina's special friends, overlooked. Sally messed up their desks and laid out in plain sight on top of Adelaide's desk the bag of lemon drops she found concealed under a tablet. Not that she disapproved of having candy in school, provided you could get away with it; she only disapproved of Adelaide's never offering anyone else a piece. For a moment she considered tampering with the clock, but it was too high up on the wall to be reached by standing on a chair. Besides, the bell was already beginning to ring for half past eight.

At the conclusion of the geography class Miss Clancey requested Sally to carry a note to the second floor. Sally thought she had never been so glad to be sent on an errand. She was so restless she couldn't sit still. The desk had shrunk, the wood hardened, until she couldn't make herself comfortable no matter how she arranged herself. It was a great relief to be able to stretch her legs.

She took the steps two at a time, pausing at the landing to slide down the banister and take the steps all over again, for sheer need of activity. The note delivered, she walked the length of the upper corridor to return by the farther staircase.

The farther staircase led down below the first floor where Sally's room was, to Mr. Namm's precincts. If she happened to meet him, she thought to herself, she would say she had come down the wrong steps. Which was the truth, any way you looked at it. Mr. Namm, however, was nowhere visible. Three or four little boys from kindergarten or first grade were hovering excitedly about some object at the foot of the steps. A mouse, Sally saw it was, the tip of its tail caught in a trap.

It had been eating the fish food in their cupboard, the children competed with each other to explain, and their teacher had set a trap for it. Just a little while ago they heard the trap go *snap!* They were a committee the teacher appointed to take it to Mr. Namm, but the mouse had jumped off the cardboard on which they were holding it and every time they started to pick it up, it flopped out of reach.

Sally took charge. Two boys turned over an empty wastebasket, and the other two boys and Sally shoved the trapped creature inside, righting the basket before the mouse could escape.

"That will be all now, boys, thank you." She was surprised how much she could make her voice sound like Miss Clancey's. "You may go back to your room now. I'll attend to the mouse."

What to do with it she didn't really know. She did not like any kind of mice except white, clean ones, and she was not particularly fond of those. But she did not intend to give it to Mr. Namm, it was so scared and trembly. If she could have brought herself to hold it while she struggled to loosen its tail, she would have set it free. What difference does it make whether a mouse eats a package of fish food in a kindergarten cupboard? It's not the same as having a mouse in the kitchen pantry, not in the least the same. Maybe if she took it upstairs to the first floor she would find a boy to open the trap.

The door of the fourth grade room was slightly ajar. Above the confused noises that echoed outward, Sally heard a familiar voice. "Does everybody have a pencil?" It was Miss Bird, substituting for the regular teacher.

On tiptoe, though the hubbub within the room made such precaution unnecessary, Sally made her way through the fourth grade cloakroom to set the wastebasket beside the doorsill. Boldly she pushed the door open and stepped inside. "May I please speak to you, Miss Bird? There's something in the wastebasket."

The cloakroom was unlighted and the day overcast, but even in the semi-darkness Miss Bird recognized the object at the bottom of the basket. Had she had any doubt, the mouse itself would have dispelled it, for it chose that moment to make a violent, but fortunately unsuccessful, leap for freedom.

Miss Bird screamed. Not loudly—Miss Bird would never be other than ladylike—a shrill little staccato cry that penetrated to the farthest corners of the fourth grade room and brought the entire class charging to her rescue.

Everybody who could—a goodly majority, mostly boys—jammed into the cloakhall around the basket. Sally was momentarily swept backward against a coat hook, but she righted herself on the instant and asserted her authority as an upper grader. "Don't push, children. If you push like that, nobody can see." Some of the boys nearest her stepped back a few inches to let the others have a look.

Miss Bird's sole concern seemed to be for the mouse. "Take it away," she commanded, her voice trembling. "Take it away this instant!"

"Where, Miss Bird?" Sally waited politely for more specific instructions. "Where shall I take it?"

"I'll do it," volunteered a score of eager voices, and two-score eager hands sought possession of the quarry. "Let me! Ouch, you're pinching! You're standing on my foot, you are! Move over, before I make you!"

"You mustn't quarrel, children," Sally reminded them pacifically. "Your teacher didn't tell you to take the mouse away; she told me." The authority of superior rank and age was not without temporary effect upon the mob. "Where shall I take it, Miss Bird?"

The poor lady's nerves were on edge. "Anywhere," she rasped, "anywhere to get rid of it."

Had Sally been more conscientious (it may have been the cup of coffee rather than her conscience which was to blame) it might possibly have occurred to her to lend Miss Bird a hand in restoring order. But how the fourth grade was to be herded back into their respective seats to attend quietly to multiplication tables seemed to Sally to be Miss Bird's business, not hers.

She still did not know what to do with the mouse. For a number of minutes she stood by the great front doors of the hall, looking out into the street, wishing a boy would come along to help her with the trap. It had begun to snow. It was no kind of weather to put a mouse out in, a mouse which was in no condition to make a dash for a neighboring garage or kichen.

Sally stepped outside to cool herself off, not forgetting to take the wastebasket with her, to keep Mr. Namm from making inquiries if he should happen to stroll through the hall.

The snow was falling thicker and thicker, swirling and eddying upon drifts of wind, so softly cold against her cheeks, so fairy-white as it settled and clung to her dress, she let herself dream for a moment of turning into a snow-maiden. In her mind's eye she beheld herself transformed as she stood there, a figure so beautiful, so white and pure, that all who passed would pause to sigh, "Alas, alas, for the innocent snow-maiden!"

In imagination she heard their sighs, heard Dorothy weep with sorrow, saw her get down upon her bended knees upon the playground to beg forgiveness. The snow-maiden spoke no word, because she couldn't. But while Dorothy wept and pleaded, slowly a teardrop formed in the snow-maiden's eye, to fall sparkling like a diamond upon her snowy cheek. And by that sign Dorothy knew she was forgiven.

"Hi, Sally! What are you doing out here?" It was Max Allen, whited with snow like Sally, and two hours late for school because their furnace fire

had gone out and his father was away on business and it took forever for him and his mother to start it up again, it smoked so on account of the dampers.

He was more than willing to officiate in the release of the captive. "Let's race it, what do you say?" he inquired before he turned it loose. "I'll bet a nickel we can beat it because we take longer steps."

But the mouse got a head start and took a different route from its two competitors. They gave up the race, content to watch it streaking in a black line through the curtaining snow.

"It's making for the Balsleys'," Max reported. "They keep chickens. It'll find plenty to fatten up on at their place."

Max set the wastebasket on top of the entrance radiator to dry. "Oh, by the way, Sally," he remarked as they separated to go to their respective classrooms, "there's something I've been meaning to ask you. A couple of us fellows are going to sell orangeade and lemon squash at the bazaar Friday night. We need a girl to wash glasses in our booth. Would you be willing? You ought to bring an apron."

Sally was willing, and she had an apron. As a matter of fact she had two, and she would bring them both, in case one should get something spilled on it.

Miss Clancey sent her immediately to the girls' washroom to rub her hair with paper towels and hold her head over the radiator until hair and dress were thoroughly dried "I'll hear your explanations later," she said, loud enough for the class to hear.

Sally had not given a thought to explanations. Nor did she think about them now. As she draped herself over the radiator she was too preoccupied with the orangeade booth at the bazaar to trouble herself about how to account to Miss Clancey for an hour's absence upon a three-minute errand. She noticed absently how straight and limp the wetness made her hair. Nobody would ever believe it had been put up on curlers last night. The heat from the radiator, the quietness of the room, made her feel drowsier and drowsier, and quite at peace with the whole world, including Angelina.

When, some time later, she returned to the classroom, Miss Clancey summoned her to the desk. "Did you deliver my note to Miss Acree?"

"Yes, Miss Clancey, I delivered it right away." Sally spoke in a low voice, not because she was afraid to speak up but because she was so sleepy she didn't feel like carrying on a conversation.

"Then what did you do?"

"There was a mouse," she replied vaguely.

"Did the mouse chase you outdoors, Sarah?" If Miss Clancey was being sarcastic, Sally was beyond caring. She was only a trifle surprised that a teacher would ask so ridiculous a question.

"Miss Bird said to get rid of it." Sally had difficulty stifling a yawn. She didn't believe ever in her whole life she'd had such a hard time staying awake. "But it ran away."

"Did you try to catch it?"

"Not very hard," said Sally, remembering how soon she and Max had given up the race with the mouse.

When the class was putting on wraps to go home, Miss Clancey took Sally aside. She mustn't return to school this afternoon, Miss Clancey said kindly; her cheeks were flushed and she might be a little feverish. Her mother ought to put her to bed. Nor was she to worry about homework. Maybe she had been studying too hard.

Chapter 7

A Torn Sleeve

On the evening of the church bazaar, the first thing on the program was Dorothy's play. It was so loudly applauded the cast had to take two curtain calls. A little later, still in costume, they cooled themselves off with orangeade at Max's booth.

Dorothy was surprised, and somewhat impressed, to see who was washing glasses behind the counter. "Hello, Sally," she called in greeting, "meet my friends," but she did not tell their names or say who Sally was. The success of the play may have made her forget that Sally was still almost a newcomer. Her gilded cardboard crown and great necklace of brass curtain rings (if you didn't know, you'd think they were pure gold), the flow-

ing cape her mother had fashioned from an old blue velvet curtain, and the royal way she carried her head gave her the appearance of a veritable princess. No wonder Tim Atkins, who was tending the stand with Max, spent so much time talking to her Max had to remind him to fill the other girls' glasses.

Business prospered. The Sunday-school basement where the bazaar was installed was crowded and everyone seemed to be thirsty. The bevy of actresses was succeeded by a crowd of boys, some of whom ordered two drinks; to be followed in turn by several girls. As Sally swished the tumblers up and down in the soapsuds, rinsing them under a faucet, it was fun to listen to the conversations. More than once she laughed to herself at jokes the boys made. The girls were inclined rather to gossip than to nonsense. One of them mentioned Dorothy, adding "She's pretty, isn't she?"

"Yes, but she knows it. And she's cliquey." (The girl pronounced it "clicky," as Sally used to before Gran corrected her.) "I don't like people who act as if they're better than anyone else."

Sally almost choked with indignation. If she hadn't had her hands in water, and if Max and Tim hadn't been standing there (she hoped they hadn't heard), she would have told the girl what she thought of her for saying things like that about Dorothy. She was jealous, that was what the girl was, jealous because Dorothy was so pretty and popular. But mixed with the desire to defend Dorothy and a sense of outrage that anyone should presume to criticize her, was another feeling. In some remote part of Sally's mind a voice whispered that what the girl said was true. Sally tried to ignore the whisper, but it was too insistent to be dismissed unheard. It made her feel disloyal, uncomfortable, guilty.

Even when some of Don's friends laid down their money on the counter and called for lemon squash, the sense of guilt persisted. But at Skids Cassidy's peremptory demand to be served by the "lady," else he'd take his trade to the fishpond, Sally forgot her discomfort of mind. Skids and Shorty both invited her to a treat. She accepted Skids' invitation because he asked her first. She took a lemon squash, with two straws, because she had never had it before, and drank it all, not to appear impolite, though she did not enjoy the taste.

Don made believe to threaten Skids and Shorty because they had cut in on his best girl, but Sally made peace among them by promising to have a chocolate soda with them at the drugstore some day. Then the boys settled down to a sober discussion of the odds in the coming basketball game. It was gratifying to be sitting in the center of the discussion, especially gratifying for a girl who had not only played basketball herself but had been elected captain of her team. Business being slack, Max and Tim leaned elbows on the counter beside Sally to listen too.

Afterward Max told Tim to take a turn at dishwashing, to give Sally a rest. She didn't need one, she protested, but there's no denying it proved more diverting to exchange remarks with customers and make sales than to wash dishes. To Father's offer somewhat later to take over the counter while the three fished in the fishpond and made the rounds of the other booths, only Tim yielded. Both Sally and Max preferred to stick to business. Max had already taken in three dollars and fifteen cents; he hoped to make it a full fiver before closing time.

Father treated Miss Clancey and Ellen Gates' mother to an orangeade and paid double. Sally was proud of Father, he looked so dressed up in his best suit. Once or twice during the evening she caught a glimpse of Angelina and Adelaide, but they did not come near the booth. Sally supposed Angelina was still sulky because she had hung her wraps on Angelina's hook. Let her sulk; it wouldn't put anybody's nose out of joint except her own.

The crowd had diminished, many of the booths were sold out, and not more than three or four bottles remained in Max's stock of soft drinks when Don's mother brought several of her friends from the apron and baked goods counters to refresh themselves at the orangeade stand.

"I didn't know you had two daughters," remarked Mrs. Hopkins. "I believe Sally resembles you more than your other daughter."

Mrs. Brown slipped her arm across Sally's shoulders. "Sally and her brother Don are like me in coloring. And Sally's like me in disposition too. We're both inclined to take people as we find them, aren't we, daughter?"

"Yes, Mother," murmured Sally, half shy, half proud. A most wonderful warm feeling slid over her as she said the word, as if joy glancing into the deeps of her mind made summer sunshine there.

Mrs. Brown and Father waited while Max and Sally washed the last few glasses and stacked them in boxes ready for the janitor. Tim had not returned, which meant they had to do his share of cleaning too.

"He's not always dependable when there's work to be done," Max commented. "But he's tops in baseball, and when he says a thing is true you can bet your bottom dollar on it."

Sally's happiness at hearing her new mother say they resembled each other had kept her from thinking what it meant to be "inclined to take people as we find them." Now, however, she turned the expression over in her mind, because it seemed to fit Max's disposition too. He wasn't mad at Tim for shirking, and his feelings hadn't been hurt because Tim would rather have fun at the fishpond with somebody else than stay in the booth with Max. He liked Tim anyhow, because Tim was a good athlete and always told the truth.

Gran always said everybody had a few faults; you couldn't expect them not to, at least not until they got to heaven. The important thing was to make allowance for other people's shortcomings and try to get rid of your own. Sally didn't believe she had ever really understood before what Gran meant by "making allowance." . . . Gran would like Max. Maybe next summer they could invite him to visit them in Westfield.

It was ten minutes of twelve when the family got home. The neighbor who had been sitting up with Bobby was so sound asleep in a chair she didn't hear them come in. If they had been burglars they could have carried her off, they teased her, but she said they'd have dropped her like a hot potato before they'd gone far.

Dorothy passed the paper bag of walnut divinity she had bought at the bazaar, insisting that Sally take two pieces so she'd have one to eat while she got ready for bed. It seemed to Sally quite the most delectable confection she had ever tasted, meltingly sweet and creamy white and rich with nutmeats.

It was not until the next evening at supper that Father remembered to tell what Miss Clancey had said when he inquired about Sally's school work. She didn't belong in that section, in Miss Clancey's opinion; she ought to be transferred into the advanced group. And she would be too, if Miss Clancey had any influence with Mr. Armitage. There was one thing, however, which made Miss Clancey hesitate about taking the matter up with the principal.

Something caught in Sally's throat, but whether it was too hasty a swallow of baked potato or a kind of knot that rose up inside her throat to meet the potato before it could slide down, it would be impossible to say. Her deportment! It must be her deportment on Wednesday morning, letting the mouse escape instead of turning it over to Mr. Namm, and not going directly back to her own room after the note was delivered. Miss Clancey must have told Father that on account of the immaturity of Sally's deportment (it is a phrase teachers always use when they mean you don't behave yourself) she ought to be retained in the slow section until she could learn to conduct herself with appropriate maturity.

It might take all the rest of the year to prove to Miss Clancey that she didn't always act like that. And in the meantime she would have to stay on in the same class with Angelina who used your pencils and broke the points, and borrowed your paper and didn't pay it back, and copied your answers and didn't wash her neck clean. It was a prospect too drear to be faced with equanimity.

But Miss Clancey had not told Father anything of the kind. She said, Father continued, righting Bobby's glass of milk just in time to keep it from spilling over into Bobby's lap, Miss Clancey said she was somewhat anxious lest Sally was not getting to bed early enough. Only a few mornings ago she had seemed to be in a daze for lack of sleep. Miss Clancey feared she was studying too late at night. If promoting her into the other section would mean staying up later and later, Miss Clancey could not with a clear conscience recommend the promotion.

"I wonder what ever gave her the idea that Sally wasn't getting enough sleep." Mrs. Brown was puzzled. "Almost before her light's turned off, she's asleep, and her room is dark long before Dorothy's."

"Sometimes the rooms get too hot, and you can't open the windows because there's a thermostat and the janitor comes up and complains." Dorothy contributed her interpretation of Miss Clancey's misapprehension. "I can hardly keep my eyes open myself sometimes."

"That must be it," said Father. "I hadn't observed that there was anything wrong with Sally's health."

Sally didn't say anything. There was nothing for her to say, especially since she didn't wish to mention the Dr. Jekyll-ish and Mr. Hyde-ish cup of coffee, on Don's account. She felt grateful to Dor othy for taking her part.

"Well, I presume we ought to tell Miss Clancey we'll see to it Sally goes to bed early if she's promoted," Father continued. "Will you call her up, Julia, or shall I?" He seemed relieved to have his wife say she'd attend to it, as soon as school opened Monday morning.

It was Tuesday, however, before Sally entered the other class. After school on Monday Miss Clancey took her up to the principal's office. Mr. Armitage asked her some history and geography questions and gave her a few arithmetic problems to solve. Then he made a little talk about how gratified he was to receive such a good report of her and how he hoped she would continue to show herself a diligent and conscientious student in Miss Johnson's room. Sally promised she would, but since she was exerting herself all the while to look particularly wide awake, perhaps she did not pay so close attention to his homily as it deserved.

Only Angelina and her two satellites seemed to begrudge Sally her advancement. At recess they strolled past the little knot of girls from Miss Johnson's room who were debating whether or not to start a game of fox and geese. Angelina brushed against Sally. "Think you're smart, don't you?" she muttered.

Sally pretended not to hear. "Hello, girls," she said, but none of the three acknowledged her greeting.

Angelina stuck her nose in the air. "Some people are too smart for their own good," she remarked spitefully, but whether to Sally or Adelaide was not clear.

Sally turned her back. If that was how Angelina wanted things to be, Sally wouldn't have anything more to do with her. Nevertheless she could not help feeling somewhat uncomfortable. It isn't pleasant to know somebody holds a grudge against you.

A day or two later, Sally and Angelina met again. Miss Johnson had kept Sally after school for a test on some make-up work in history which Miss Clancey's class had not yet studied. It was growing dusk, the playground was deserted, and a slow drizzle was freezing on the sidewalk. Sally was wondering whether she had omitted any of the chief effects of the cotton gin, in *Question 2,* and trying in spite of the slipperiness to run because the rain was wet and she had no umbrella, when

Angelina and Jessie loomed out of the semi-darkness in front of her.

"Hello, Jessie," she said. "Hello, Angelina."

"Smart aleck! Think you're awful smart, don't you? Playing up to old Clancey to get her to promote you!"

Sally would have hurried on past Angelina, but the two blocked her way. She waited, there being nothing else she could do. In spite of herself she felt somewhat uneasy.

"Think you can insult people, don't you, making marks on their spelling papers for everyone to see?" continued Angelina, drawing closer. "Think you can take their coat hooks away from them, don't you?" Her voice was menacing.

Sally made another attempt to slip past her. She was not really afraid, but neither did she feel particularly reckless. When it's getting so dark you can't see very well, two people look like rather a crowd, especially if one of them is a head taller than you are.

"No, you don't!" Angelina stretched out both arms as wide as they would go to block Sally's passage, and Jessie stretched out her hands too.

"Not one step till you've got down on your bended knees and said you're sorry. When people insult me, they have to apologize. People don't take liberties with Angelina Tubbs and not live to regret it." Her grammar was somewhat askew, but the meaning was plain.

Sally was beginning to chafe at the stoppage. She wasn't sorry she had used Angelina's hook (it wasn't hers anyhow, it belonged to the school) and she regretted even less that she had put a big red question mark on Angelina's spelling paper. If she had it to do over, she would do the same again. And make the question mark bigger, too!

"Let me alone," she said. "Get out of my way. I want to go home."

Angelina and Jessie moved a step closer, Jessie slightly to the rear of her chieftain. "Oh, you do, do you? Well, you're not going till I say you can."

Sally began to count to herself—*one, two*—very slowly. It was Gran's remedy to keep your temper from boiling over and saying things you might be sorry for afterward. Sally didn't always remember about the remedy in time to profit from it, but the freezing rain, the gathering dusk, and the way the shadows made Angelina (and even mousey Jessie) appear larger than normal combined to remind her that discretion sometimes serves better than force.

"Who do you think you are, anyhow?" Angelina continued, edging nearer. (*Three, four*) "I wouldn't be caught dead in that coat" (*five, six*) "your old stepmother makes you wear!"

"She's not old, she's younger than your mother,

so there!" Sally cried hotly. "And she'd get me a new coat if I asked her, too!"

Angelina laughed, a slow, slurring laugh that made Sally's cheeks burn, her throat choke with anger. "Whyn't you ask her?"

"Because I don't want to, that's why." Sally attempted to push her way past the double barrier.

"Oh, no, you don't!" Angelina seized her by the arm, twisting it back until an almost unendurable sharp pain shot up to the shoulder. "You'll stay right here till—"

Sally struck out with her other arm, blindly, with all her strength. The blow took Angelina full on the chin. She grabbed at Sally, clutched her coat sleeve as she started to run, lost her footing on the icy walk and fell, dragging Sally down with her. In the tangle of arms and legs Sally hardly knew which were hers, which Angelina's, but she worked one arm free to pound against Angelina's chest.

"Jessie," Angelina yelled for her henchman, "help me, Jessie."

"Keep away, Jessie," Sally warned breathlessly. "I don't want to have to hurt you."

She was on top now, she had extricated both feet. As soon as she could pull her other arm free from her opponent's viselike clutch the victory would be hers. Jessie, who was apparently not the stuff of which martyrs are made, took two steps backward to compensate for the single step she had advanced, and stood whimpering in the rain.

Sally summoned strength for a violent jerk of her captive arm. There was a sound of ripping cloth, an inarticulate ejaculation, half squeal, half squall, from Angelina, and Sally struggled triumphantly to her feet. To avoid the appearance of too precipitate haste, she brushed off the front of her coat. She ought to say something, she ought to let Angelina know what she thought of her. But what to say? She couldn't think of a thing, she was still so out of breath.

"The next time you pick on someone, Angelina Tubbs" (it's not easy to make your voice sound cool and collected when you are breathing hard, but Sally thought she managed it rather well) "you'd better pick on somebody your own size."

The words were scarcely spoken before she realized to her chagrin how inappropriate a remark it was. That was what you ought to say when you rescued someone from a bully. Half a block further on, however, the comment began to seem altogether fitting. For Angelina acually was taller than she. Angelina would think she was being sarcastic. Sally couldn't help feeling pleased with herself at the wittiness of her parting shot.

Even virtue triumphant cannot remain forever immune to drizzle and cold and murky gloom. By the end of the following block Sally's exhilaration had ebbed away, her elation faded. Her hands were like icicles (she didn't know what had become of her gloves), her feet heavy as lead, and her arm was aching where Angelina had twisted it. Worse, there was a churning sensation inside her that might mean she was going to be sick at her stomach.

She stopped stock-still and took three deep breaths, careful to breathe through her nose though it felt a little bruised and swollen. Fresh air is good for a queasy stomach. . . . What would her new mother say when she saw the state her clothes were in? And Dorothy? If only she could slip into the house and upstairs without anyone's noticing!

Dorothy and her mother were both in the kitchen as Sally sought to edge past the door, Mrs. Brown frying chops and rolling out biscuits for supper while Dorothy finished scraping carrots for salad.

"Hi, Sally, where've you been all this time?" Dorothy greeted her. "It's almost six o'clock."

"Miss Johnson gave me a history test." If anybody said anything about how she looked, Sally didn't think she could bear it.

"You got caught in the rain, I see," commented her mother, with scarcely more than a glance in her direction. "Better get out of those wet clothes as fast as you can, before you catch cold. Dorothy, run up and turn the hot water on in the tub, so Sally can warm herself up with a quick dip before dinner. And hurry, both of you!"

Dorothy was sitting on the edge of Sally's bed when Sally came warm and clean and still a trifle dampish from the bathroom. "What happened, Sally?" she wanted to know.

"Here, I'll help you make a straight parting in the back." She took the comb from Sally. "Did you get into a fight?"

Sally nodded. She could see Dorothy's face in the mirror. Dorothy didn't look the least bit mortified or put out with her. She looked just plain curious.

"With Angelina Tubbs," Sally informed her briefly.

"What about?"

"I guess maybe she didn't like it because I got promoted and she didn't."

Whether she had learned from living in the house with an older brother or from her own experience, Dorothy knew it requires something more immediate to one's pride and honor than a school promotion to spark a combat. "Really truly, Sally, what was it?"

"Angelina said I had an old stepmother."

"Oh," said Dorothy, and again, slowly, "oh," and then, "I wish I'd been there!" Sally saw in the mirror that her face was flushed deep red.

Her mother called her to carry the salad plates to the dining room and take up the peas before the mashed potatoes got cold. Hastily Sally pulled a fresh dress over her head and stooped to tie her shoes. Dorothy wouldn't have let Angelina make insulting remarks about her mother either: she would have fought too. Dorothy might have a few shortcomings, but as Gran always said, people wouldn't be human if they didn't have faults. And Dorothy was spunky; she'd have given Angelina as good as she got, or better. Sally liked people who had enough spunk to stand up for what was right.

Later, when Sally showed her mother where she

had torn her coat sleeve, Mrs. Brown said she
had been thinking of getting her a new coat anyhow. Lewis and Emerson's was advertising such
unusual savings on girls' coats they really ought to
take advantage of the sale.

Chapter 8

The Pole Vault

Miss Johnson's and Miss Clancey's classes were planning a track meet to earn money for the Red Cross. A few boys had campaigned to hold it outdoors where there would be more room for a display of skill and daring, but March winds and March mud and March rains and snow flurries campaigned against them. By a large majority both classes voted to stage it in the gymnasium.

Sally was on the art committee, to make posters announcing the meet as well as signs to inform spectators of the order of events. For almost a month the committee had been at work, and now only one sign remained unlettered. Sally had brought it home to finish because tomorrow it would be needed. Ink, pencils, crayons, ruler, cardboard, scissors and eraser spread out at one end of the dining table, she bent herself to her task. It gave her particular pleasure to make the letters stand out sharp and clear, as free of smudges as though they had come from a printer's shop, for it was the sign for the pole vault.

Only three girls were entered in the pole vault, and she was one of the three. The others were all boys, some of them quite tall boys. She was entered in one of the relay races also, but so were almost all the other girls, since everybody had to participate in two events and most girls were better at running than at technical feats like rope-climbing and tumbling.

Not until she entered Miss Johnson's group had Sally tried vaulting, but long training with stilts in Gran's big back yard had made her familiar with the possibilities which poles offer for balancing in mid-air. Miss Jones, the gymnasium teacher (they all called her "Jonesey" because they liked her), had showed her where to place her hands and how to slide the lower hand along the pole toward the upper one for the take-off, and had superintended the trials until she learned how. Thereafter only practice was needed. Had it been possible, Sally would have practiced hours on end, day after day. Not only did she wish to win points for her class—even if she came in third it would mean points—but vaulting was fun.

The few running steps with the pole loosely balanced in her hands, the momentary half-pause while she brought the lower end to position on the thick canvas mat, the pull up with both hands, and then the soaring upward swing, weightless as though upborne on wings, up, up, and over the bar, to land safe and sound on the canvas mattress beyond the hurdle—even in her sleep she re-lived the buoyant movement, the gladdening sense of flight. Sometimes she waked herself up with a start, dreaming she must brace herself for the landing. Sometimes she dreamed she won the competition, sometimes she dreamed she lost.

Though not for anything would she have let anyone know, she was determined to come in first, to give the family reason to be proud of her. Father had bought tickets for them all, including himself, although it was such a busy time of year with the approach of gardening time and customers needing spades and hoes and wire fencing, he would not be able to get away from the store.

Nor could Don attend the meet, since he must

play forward in a game that very same Friday afternoon. Were it not the last game of the season, he would have been tempted to let them put a sub in his place. Sally would never have permitted it, not for an instant, she told him; a high school basketball game is important.

When he came to Westfield to visit, she would demonstrate in Gran's back yard how high she could go. He thought she could probably vault even higher there. A pole has more secure purchase on the ground than on a gym mat.

Sally's mother intended to pay the two extra dimes it would cost for her and Bobby to sit in the reserved section, where the view was best. She was upstairs now with Bobby, doctoring him so he wouldn't catch cold from the drenching he had got playing in a puddle. Bobby was drawn as irresistibly to puddles as ocean tides to the moon.

Whether or not Dorothy, who was spending the night with Mildred, would come to the meet was anybody's guess. She had remarked yesterday that "it all depended." Upon what, she did not specify, but Sally supposed she would not come unless Mildred was willing.

Though Dorothy had been increasingly friendly of late, inviting Sally to a motion picture when

Mildred wasn't along and showing a marked interest in descriptions of the good times everyone had in Westfield during summer vacation—picnicking and going camping out by the river and riding horseback at Uncle Tracy's farm—Sally could not count on her. At least she could not count on her for sure. But if she hadn't gone to stay all night with Mildred, Sally was practically positive she would have come to the meet tomorrow. Maybe she would anyhow. It was a hope built upon longing rather than upon trust.

The lettering for the placard was finished. There remained only the edges to be trimmed straight, an occasional thumb or finger mark to erase. In the living room where Don was studying, Sally could hear the rustle of Father's newspaper as he turned the sheet.

"Mr. Cassidy tells me his son is going to study law at college."

Sally had noticed that whenever Father was alone with Don he brought up the subject of college. Don had not yet taken the scholarship examinations, and he didn't want anyone, not even his mother, to know. There would be time enough to tell after he had passed them, he told Sally. And if he didn't pass, why, then he wouldn't be obliged to explain anything to anyone. What people didn't know wouldn't hurt them.

Father ought to be able to guess that Don did not wish to discuss college, for he always made some excuse as soon as he could to leave the room. Maybe that was why he and Father never made jokes with each other. Maybe Don thought Father ought to keep still about college.

"I should think you would be as ambitious as the Cassidy boy," Father continued. "Surely you can't believe you will be satisfied to clerk in a store all your life, Don."

There it was again! Sally couldn't help feeling a little impatient with Father. He had no right to think Don wasn't ambitious. Don had lots more ambition than Skids Cassidy. He intended to be an engineer and build bridges, not little bridges over country creeks, but great spans across mighty rivers like the Mississippi and the Amazon. That was why he crammed trig. Engineers must know all there is to know about mathematics.

Sally was proud of Don, he got such high marks on his tests. It made her study arithmetic harder. Until Don told her, she had never realized how important arithmetic is.

"Perhaps not, sir." A few minutes later Sally

heard Don go upstairs. She hoped his feelings had not been hurt.

For some reason—it may have been the stillness in the room or something like homesickness or loneliness within her own mind—she thought for the first time about Father's feelings. She wondered if they had been hurt, too. Something Gran had said came back to her, something about her mother, that other mother whom Sally could not quite remember. She had helped Father see things through her eyes. Gran trusted Sally to help him too. Perhaps if he understood about the scholarship he would feel better.

But Don didn't want anyone to know. The only reason he had told Sally was because she had unlocked the door that Sunday night and given him her piece of chocolate cake and loaned him her two dollars to buy his mother a birthday gift. He might not like it if she told Father. Though she hadn't promised, Don would expect her to keep his secret to herself. She felt responsible for Don. But if Father ought to know . . . She was responsible for Father too.

Slowly she gathered up the crayons and eraser, scissors and placard. Father did not look up when she appeared in the doorway. "Want to see the sign I made, Father?" She tried to sound lively.

He laid down his paper to admire the placard, but he was thinking about something else. "It's for the indoor track meet," she explained.

"I see, I see. That's fine." She could tell he was hardly paying attention although he was looking at the sign. She noticed how tired he looked, or maybe sad. Perhaps he felt lonesome this evening too, like her. Perhaps Don had hurt his feelings without meaning to.

"Now I have to do my homework." She lingered, trying to make conversation. He might think she was interfering if she spoke straight out about Don. "It's compound interest, four problems. Miss Johnson usually assigns more, but not this time, because of the meet." She wasn't getting anywhere; Father was still thinking about something else, he still looked lonesome.

"Don says arithmetic is important for girls too," she continued hastily before Father should return to his newspaper. "Of course it's more important for engineers. That's what Don's going to be, and build bridges. He's going to study engineering in college."

Father was paying attention now. If only he

would ask questions, to help her out! But he didn't; he only kept looking at her. "That's why Don studies trig so hard. He's trying to win a scholarship so it won't cost you anything."

"Does Don believe I would be unwilling to pay?" There was so strange an expression on Father's face Sally was almost afraid she had said something she shouldn't.

"Oh, no, I don't think so," she sought to reassure him. "He says there's not much profit in a hardware store and he ought to look after himself." She was afraid she was bungling things, Father still looked at her so fixedly. "Don's proud. He doesn't want to be an expense to anybody." Maybe it had been a mistake to tell Father. Maybe she had made things worse. She wished she had gone upstairs and done her homework and hadn't spoken to Father.

"I misunderstood the situation," he said slowly, more to himself than to her. "I'll have to make things right with Don."

And then he smiled at Sally, the sudden, warm, exciting way Gran smiled when something that went wrong at first, began to go right. It was as if, as she met his eyes, he was telling her something she had longed all these past weeks to hear—that she and Father belonged to each other in a different way from any others of the family. There was no need for them to speak it in words. They understood each other.

"Unless I do my 'rithmetic problems Miss Johnson'll demote me back into the retarded section!" A kind of embarrassment sent her dashing up the stairs, to dance a jig on tiptoe in the privacy of her own room before she took out her arithmetic book. And even then, it took her a long time to settle down.

There was slight reason for rejoicing the next afternoon, however. At the hour for the track meet to begin, not a single member of the Brown family was on hand to see Sally take part. Of course she had not expected Father or Don, but she had expected her mother and Bobby. But the puddle was exacting its price, and Bobby's mother had no choice but to stay at home and keep him in bed until his temperature went down.

Until the last minute Sally clung to the hope that Dorothy would appear. Dorothy had not referred to the meet at lunchtime, and Sally was too independent to remind her again. If she would not come of her own accord, Sally would not beg her. Nevertheless hope persisted that Dorothy was planning to surprise her, or that perhaps she might have forgotten about the pole vault but would remember before it was too late.

Miss Jones blew her whistle for contestants to line up for the first race. Sally stood against a wall ladder with Ellen and Jean and a group of other girls who were entered in a later race. While the runners got on their marks, poised for the signal, Sally's eyes searched the bleachers, row by row, hoping to see what she knew she would not see—Dorothy's wine-red coat and Dorothy's blond hair and Dorothy's blue eyes looking for Sally among the girls in gym suits waiting their turns in the background. The gym door opened to admit an occasional late-comer, but it was never Dorothy.

For a while Sally felt so discouraged she almost made up her mind not to make any effort to win the pole vault. Other people's families thought enough of them to come, but not hers. Probably she was the only person in the whole two classes who didn't have anyone belonging to her in the audience. Nobody had come on purpose to watch her take part. It wouldn't make any difference whether she came in first or last. Nobody would care.

Pride came to her rescue, pride and a will too

sturdy to be balked by disheartenment. Even if nobody cared but herself whether she won or lost, she cared. She cared tremendously. And she would try her level best. Even supposing Sam and Jim should jump higher than she, as well they might because their long legs gave them such an advantage in the take-off, she ought to be able to come in third. If she tried hard enough she might come in second, or maybe first.

The crowd kept increasing, mostly boys from other grades who had to stand because the bleachers were filled. Max Allen called out, "Hi, Sally! I'm betting on you!"

"Better not!" she called in return. "You might lose!" But she didn't mean it.

As the meet progressed, and race succeeded race, and rope-climbing and tumbling and high-jumping followed the races, and winners and losers were applauded, the time for the pole vault approached. Miss Jones sent the vaulting entrants to line up at the other end of the gym. As Sally passed along the bleachers she heard a voice saying, "I almost didn't get here, I had so much to do."

It was Dorothy. It was Dorothy herself sitting squeezed in between two girls Sally wasn't ac-

quainted with. Now she must win, she must and
she would! She might have been treading a daisy-
starred meadow, there was such a sudden springi-
ness under her feet.

The first five or six contestants were soon elimi-
nated, two of them at the first try. Sally wished
she could follow Sam and Jim, to know before
she made her trial how high they vaulted. But
Miss Jones had put the two tallest boys last in the
line. Sally was fifth from last, just in front of
Aaron Bates, a tall boy, but rather clumsy. When
her number was called she held the pole lightly
balanced, and kept her eyes on the bar she must
hurdle. The bar was set low, as for all first trials,
but unless you were careful and kept your head
you might miss even on a low bar. Sally had no
intention of missing. Nor did she let the applause
as she flew over the bar make her feel cocky. The
real trial was yet to come.

Once, twice, three times, four times, the height
of the bar was increased, and each time Sally sur-
mounted it. The fourth time the applause was thun-
derous, for no one else had vaulted so high. "Rah,
rah, rah! Sal-ly, Sal-ly!" From lofty ceiling and
wide brick walls of the great room the chanting
cry re-echoed. "Sal-ly, rah for Sal-ly Brown!"

But the contest was not yet won. There remained one notch more for the bar to be raised. Beyond that Miss Jones would not permit it to be lifted, for a gym floor and gym mats and mattresses are less secure than soft turf. Miss Jones did not believe in risking accidents. And anyhow this was quite high enough. At least it had been high enough to prove the undoing of the only two boys besides Jim and Sam whom Sally had reason to regard as formidable rivals.

Sally grinned an acknowledgment of the applause, and shoved her hair back out of her eyes. One braid had come undone, but there wasn't time even to catch it back with an elastic band. She was so hot she was panting, her cheeks burned, and yet the back of her neck felt chilly as if she were scared. She was not scared, however. Part of her was excited, jubilant; but her underneath self was steady, cautious and, above all, determined to do her level best.

Ready for the final take-off, pole in hand, she measured with her eyes the distance from floor to crossbar. Not only must she clear the bar, she must land on her feet. She drew a deep breath, leaned slightly forward, and pulled herself up with both hands into the air.

A moment later the floor had sprung away beneath her, the pole was lifting her lightly into the air, and like an arrow freed from the bow she went arching over the bar with a good inch or two in the clear to spare. She staggered a little on landing, but did not lose her balance. She had made it! Made it, with Dorothy there to see!

Hardly aware of the clapping, the shouts and cheers, Sally straightened up to glance back along the bleachers to find Dorothy, to see how surprised and pleased she must be at Sally's triumph. There was no Dorothy there to see. The place where she had sat was empty. She had not been interested, she had not cared enough to wait till it came Sally's turn to vault. Like a weight the thought sank into Sally's mind.

Before she could realize the full measure of her disappointment, something struck swiftly against her from the side. Her knees crumpled under the unexpected blow, pitching her forward, beyond the cushioning mattress. Her forehead struck against the floor.

Without waiting for the bar to be lowered as the rules required, indeed without waiting for his number to be called, Aaron Bates had seized the pole and made an attempt to match Sally's achieve-

ment. Perhaps it was the apparent ease of her accomplishment which inspired him to the risk, or perhaps it was the excitement of applause and cheers. Or it may have been a desire to show off.

Whatever it was, he failed to reach the bar. The upright standards wobbled as the pole crashed against them, and he and the crossbar toppled together upon Sally.

Miss Jones lifted Sally to her feet, stanching her nosebleed with a handkerchief until Miss Johnson could hurry across to take her to the locker room. Sally insisted there was nothing the matter with her, she would be all right in just a minute, but Miss Johnson was not convinced. After the nosebleed was checked she made her lie flat on a cot in Miss Jones' office to rest. Nor was she to get up until Miss Johnson or Miss Jones returned to give permission.

Sally was relieved to have Miss Johnson go, relieved to be left alone with her aching head and churning stomach and the painful memory of Dorothy's defection. She did not want to see anyone, to have to make conversation with anybody. She couldn't, she just couldn't, she felt too miserable. There was no use trying ever again to be real friends with Dorothy. Dorothy didn't want to be, she only acted as if she did sometimes when she was in a good humor. . . . Perhaps when Gran got back from California Father would let Sally go home to live with Gran again.

The shock of the fall must have made Sally drowse from time to time, for sounds of the meet echoed but intermittently in her ears. When Miss Johnson returned an hour or so later to announce that the meet had ended in a margin of victory for Sally's class, and everyone had gone home except the squad of boys helping Mr. Namm clean up, Sally crawled out from under the rough brown blanket and limped to the locker room to put on her dress and coat.

She was sufficiently herself again to be pleased at the news that she and Jim had tied for first place in the pole vault. Jim was in Miss Clancey's room. If Sally hadn't come in first too, Miss Johnson said, Miss Clancey's room would have had more points than theirs.

Miss Johnson offered to walk home with Sally, but Sally would not let her. Her mother might think she was injured, and she really wasn't. Before Miss Johnson consented to Sally's starting off alone, she made her stuff some cotton up her nose. With such a pretty dark red coat, it would be unwise not to take precautions against another nosebleed.

The lower corridor was deserted, the light beginning to fade. Sally pulled her hat down a little further to hide the lump on her forehead, and then pushed slowly down on the bar that opened the door from the inside when the night lock was on. As the door swung open, a figure darted toward her from the shadowy outer step.

"Sally, oh, Sally!" Dorothy was sobbing. "Are you all right, Sally?" She threw her arms around Sally's shoulders, holding her tight.

"Why, Dorothy," said Sally, and again because she was so astonished she could think of nothing else to say, "why, Dorothy! I thought you went home before the pole vault."

"I changed places so I could see better." Dorothy rubbed away the tears with her arm. "And then when that old Aaron Bates knocked you down and I was afraid your bones were broken and Miss Jones wouldn't let me go near where you were—"

She could not finish the sentence. No one who had been crying and worrying all alone in the dusk as long as Dorothy had, would have been able immediately to gain control of her voice. Sally patted her on the shoulder, the way she patted Rufus when he had hurt his paw.

"I told Miss Jones she hadn't any right not to let me, but she wouldn't listen." The sniffles were diminishing, the words were more articulate.

"Even when I explained that you were my sister, my very own sister, she wouldn't."

"She will next time," promised Sally, the gaiety of her tone somewhat muffled by the wads of cotton. "She'll have to, because we'll both tell her!"

"She's not so bad, really," Dorothy admitted, as arm in arm the two cut across the playground toward home, "but sometimes she's bossy. I don't like to be bossed, do you, Sally?"

Sister—my sister, my very own sister— The word shone like a star in the forest of Sally's thought, steadfast and clear.